Moses Gaster

Two Unknown Hebrew Versions of Tobit

Moses Gaster

Two Unknown Hebrew Versions of Tobit

ISBN/EAN: 9783337728694

Printed in Europe, USA, Canada, Australia, Japan

Cover: Foto ©Andreas Hilbeck / pixelio.de

More available books at **www.hansebooks.com**

TWO
UNKNOWN HEBREW VERSIONS

OF

TOBIT.

Published for the first time,

WITH INTRODUCTION AND TRANSLATION,

BY

M. GASTER, Ph.D.

———◆◆◆———

LONDON:

HARRISON AND SONS, ST MARTIN'S LANE,

Printers in Ordinary to Her Majesty.

1897.

TWO UNKNOWN HEBREW VERSIONS OF THE TOBIT LEGEND.

[Published for the First Time.]

By Dr. M. Gaster.

Reprinted from the " Proceedings of the Society of Biblical Archæology."

I.—INTRODUCTION.

Of all the Apocrypha of the Old Testament the legend of Tobit alone may be said to have come down to us in the greatest variety of texts and translations. There are no less than three more or less different Greek texts, which are not slight alterations of one and the same original, but differ often in essential points. Then there are two distinct classes of Latin translations: one the Vetus Latin, represented by a variety of texts, and agreeing in some points with the so-called Greek Sinaiticus (C), and the translation of Jerome, *i.e.*, the *Vulgate.* We have then at least two Syriac translations, both however imperfect, each of these representing a somewhat different text.

Up to a very short time ago only two Hebrew texts of Tobit were known. Both had appeared for the first time in Constantinople (I possess both editions) (*a*) in 1516, and (*b*) in 1519. The first is better known as Hebræus Munsteri (H.M.), and the second as Hebræus Fagii (H.F.), after the names of these two scholars who edited them in 1542. In 1878 Dr. Neubauer published* the till then unknown Aramaic text (Ar.), and furnished thus an important

---

* The Book of Tobit, Oxford, 1878.

A

addition to the literary tradition of the Tobit legend. In the light of Dr. Neubauer's discovery the question of the relation in which the different texts stand to one another became a little more simplified, but the material thus available was not yet sufficient to clear up, for instance, the true origin of Jerome's text. The result of the investigation, conducted by many scholars, and summarised here, has not been able to establish definitely which of the various Greek texts can claim absolute priority. Noeldeke, and following him Schuerer, adopted the view propounded by Fritzsche and others. They consider the text of our LXX (A) as the most ancient and best. The other two texts (B) and (C) are, according to them, secondary developments and modifications of that oldest text. From the same text (A) originate, so we are told, (*a*) the first fragment of the Syriac ; (*b*) the Æthiopic translation ; and (*c*) the Hebrew text (HF) ; this latter is not exactly a translation, but rather an adaptation. From the secondary Greek text, or a mixed text (B, C), arises to a certain extent (*a*) an old Aramaic text differing from that of Dr. Neubauer, which would also be more an adaptation with many characteristic changes and differences; (*b*) Vetus Lat. ; and (*c*) the second fragment of the Syriac. That supposed more complete Aramaic text now lost (*a*), is then the reputed source of the Aramaic text discovered by Dr. Neubauer (Ar.), and also of the Hebrew version of 1516 (H.M.). To the same lost Aramaic source the translation of Jerome is also traced. The net outcome of this scheme formulated by Noeldeke is that we have on the one hand the Greek text A of the LXX forming a distinct group ; and, on the other hand, a number of texts which seem to go back to one partly represented by Greek B, C, to which latter group all the Semitic versions as well as the Latin, both the Vetus and Jerome, except Syr. I, belong. Others again look to B, C as the primary source, and A as the secondary development and enlargement ; so Reusch and others.

The connection between the Latin and Aramaic-Hebrew texts, and the reasons for such marked differences between them, has not yet found an adequate explanation. Nor, to my mind, has the priority claimed for the Greek text A or for any Greek text, been established on firm ground. It is very surprising that most of the versions should favour a text (A) which, according to modern scholars, would be far from being the authentic and the oldest one, and that the authors of these numerous versions should select, as if it were, for their model, the secondary version B, C.   Still more surprising is it that the old Latin, and especially Jerome, should so completely neglect that old Greek version (A) and prefer instead, a totally different text.   Nor have we any reason to doubt Jerome's deliberate statement that he took his Tobit from an Aramaic original; Dr. Neubauer's discovery goes a long way to prove it, although Jerome's Aramaic version must have been very different from that of Dr. Neubauer.

In order to unravel the somewhat entangled skein of the numerous versions, it is advisable to start from the text of Jerome, about the date of which there cannot be any doubt.   Illgen, who has written a very elaborate and minute study on the book of Tobit,* has shown that Jerome has laid the older Latin version under considerable contribution.   According to Jerome's own statement, the text he had before him was written in Aramaic, and a Jew who knew both languages translated it to him into Hebrew, from which language he made his Latin translation.   Not a word, however, is mentioned by him of the Old Latin, and it is not a little surprising to find in his version a number of incidents and details wanting in all the others.   These additions and differences, which I will enumerate afterwards, have been lightly set down as due to his invention (Fritzsche).   I am not aware of any such liberty having been taken by Jerome with any other canonical or apocryphal book translated by him.   And although he may not have had a high respect for the Book of Tobit, it is nevertheless singular that he should have indulged in such a fanciful enlargement of a text, which he knew to be held in esteem by the Church, and that he should try to palm off his fiction as truth on the devout people who wrote to him for the book.   This, as well as his silence about the Old Latin, and the choice deliberately made by him in the selection of this version in preference to that of the LXX, call for an explanation.   This can only be found, if we assume that he had followed faithfully a text which contained those peculiar incidents and variations.   That text must have had the reputation of being the genuine version, and for that very reason had also been followed in the main by the Old Latin translation.   I do not wish to say that the Vetus Latin was translated directly from the very same text which served Jerome as a source.   Vetus Latin follows in the

---

* *Die Geschichte Tobits.* Jena, 1800.

A 2

main Greek texts, which may have been, and probably were, a Greek version of the B C type, in its turn a translation from the Aramaic, and which served thus as an intermediary source for the Old Latin. Being in the main identical with his own text, Jerome could have recourse to the Old Latin for touching up his version, which he owns to have completed in one single day. There was thus no need for him to acknowledge more than one source, namely Aramaic, as the O. Lat. was of secondary importance, and merely used by him for the purpose of rectifying the translation where it agreed with his. He took from the Old Latin, if he has taken anything at all, only materials for verbal alterations, but none of the *realia*. They agree both, because both are based upon almost one and the same text. Jerome also differs from the Vetus Latin in not a few instances, showing himself independent of it.

Having cleared the road thus far, we proceed now to the study of his original, which according to his explicit statement was Aramaic. The text published by Dr. Neubauer differs, however, in most of the peculiar incidents characteristic of the version of Jerome, and must therefore be considered merely as a faint reflex, or as a later modification of the ancient and more elaborate version. This shorter version had been incorporated into a collection of homiletical interpretations of the Pentateuch, and has suffered in consequence. This is probably the reason for the abridgement. As we shall see later on, this text has a history of its own, and by means of undoubted evidence it can be proved that it had suffered curtailment and other changes, in consequence of that connection with the Liturgy. The Hebrew text H.M. is considered to be a translation from an older and more complete Aramaic text, but it differs also in many, if not in most of the essential points, from the version of Jerome.

Before proceeding further I will point out the most important differences between Jerome and the Greek text of the LXX (A). Gr. reads *Tobit* whilst Jer. reads *Tobias*. According to Gr. Tobit was *purveyor* to the king (I, 13) ; Jer. *he has leave to go whithersoever he would* (I, 14). Gr. (I, 19) Tobit *flees alone ;* Jer. (I, 23) *he flees with his wife and child.* Gr. (II, 10) *sparrows* blind him ; Jer. *swallow.* Gr. (III, 10) Sara wishes to *strangle herself ;* Jer. *she fasts three days.* Gr. (IX, 2) the angel Raphael starts for Rages with *only one slave ;* Jer. with *four.* Gr. (XI, 14–19) Sara comes to Nineveh *the same day as Tobias ;* Jer. (XI, 14–19) after *seven days.*

The dog plays a very inferior part in Jerome, and it is not unlikely that it is a later interpolation (XI, 9). The three nights of continence are also peculiar to Jerome, not a trace of it in the Greek. Many passages that are in the Greek are missing in Jerome. Thus there is not a trace in Jerome of Tobit being maintained by Achiacharos during his blindness (II, 10), nor of the doctors attempting to cure him; and, on the other hand, not a trace can be found in the Greek of the parallel to Job (Jer. II, 12–15). The various prayers inserted in the texts are different. The wife of Reuel is called by Jerome *Hanna*, against all the other texts where she is called *Edna*. One could easily increase the number of variations, which point conclusively to a text different in many essential features from that of the LXX. Only here and there does the other text, B C, offer parallels to Jerome. The Aramaic text agrees with Jerome only in a few instances, such as the number of servants taken by the angel, the position occupied by Tobi at the court of Shalmanassar, whilst on the other hand it differs from Jerome's text in almost every other incident. The dog is not mentioned at all, and Aqiqar appears only in the commencement of the tale. Nothing better can be said of the more complete text H.M. In it there are a few other additions which are missing in the Aramaic; H.M. contains some of the same moral reflections as Jerome, and leans more towards the Greek B C than towards the Aramaic (Ar.). Another version which belongs to this cycle is the fragmentary Syriac from VII, 11, on. But this is still more remote from Jerome and from the other Aramaic text, as well as from the Greek versions in the form in which we have them. I will mention only one or two points which Syr. II has, contrary to all the rest. In XI, 13, the friends bring presents after the wedding. Tobias prays (VII, 8) for children. The angel does not say, as in the Greek (XII, 12), that he had brought the prayers before God, nor that he presents the prayers of the saints (XII, 15). On the other hand Syr. II calls the father Tobi; his friend Aqiqar; the wife of Reuel Edna, the man to whom Tobit had lent the money, is called Gabæl (Jer. Gabel).

Enough has now been said to show the great divergence that exists in not unimportant portions and incidents between the various texts belonging to this one group. Not any of these texts can, therefore, be considered as the probable direct source for the others. Neither the Aramaic, nor, so far, the Hebrew Munsteri, nor the Greek B C, nor the Syriac, though they have many points in common. And as for the Itala, and, in a higher degree, for Jerome, the resemblance between them and the others is of the slenderest nature.

What we are in search of is to find a single text, be it in Aramaic or in Hebrew, which should offer the same characteristics as the version of Jerome, without being a translation from the latter; having also its own points of divergence, so that the original character of that text should be established beyond doubt or cavil. At the same time it must have points in common with one or the other Greek text.

I think, now, that I have discovered such an ideal text, which comes up to all the requirements of the case. It is a Hebrew text copied, latest in the 13th century, from an older MS. which, if my conjecture is correct, belonged to the 11th century. In its turn, it may be, and in every probability was a copy of the original text. The MS. in the British Museum Add. 11639 is one of the finest specimens of mediæval calligraphy; it is of the choicest penmanship imaginable, and is placed among the Select on account of its artistic merits, being full of admirable illuminations and drawings. It was written by a certain Benjamin, the scribe, on very thin and perfect vellum. The larger part of the MS. is taken up by the Pentateuch, round the margin of which portions of the Hagiographa are written. Then follow prayers, poetical and liturgical compositions, laws, regulations, rules, calendar, and many other similar compositions and texts. Round some of the liturgical poems, this history of Tobit is written by the same hand and with the same care. The calendar on folio 563*b* begins with the moon-cycle 266, which corresponds to the year 5036, *i.e.*, 1276, probably the date of the writing. On folio 568*b*, however, the date 828 or 858 (= 4858) is given, which is probably the date of the original, and corresponds to the year 1068 or 1098.

The legend is written with special care; in a few places corrections are added *over* the text, and in one instance (III, 20), not having been able to read an obliterated or erased word, the scribe indicated the lacuna by dots, and did not try to correct the text. In a few instances he did not distinguish correctly the letters of the original; he writes, *e.g.*, the name of the place where Tobit and the angel went, *Dage*, instead of *Rage*. The mistake points to the form of letters in which that original, from which he copied, was written. In the Spanish and the old *Palestinian* cursive writing it is almost impossible to distinguish between D and R. I must point out, however, what cannot be a mere coincidence, that in an ancient Hebrew version of the 12th century of the longer recension of Judith discovered by me, the town (I, 5) is called *Dage*, instead of *Ragau;* absolutely identical with the Tobit text.

The text is divided in verses. At the end of Chapter VI stands the word *Half,* exactly as it is customary with sacred texts. As our text is apparently not complete at the end, this division could not be the work of the copyist, but he must have found it already in his original. I point out all these minute details, as it is necessary to convince ourselves of the fact, that we have in our MS. a *copy* of a more ancient text, and not a production of the 13th century. The contents of this new version which, for brevity's sake, I will call H.L. (Hebrew London), had so thoroughly surprised me, that I had to convince myself by the examination of all the details, and by a careful comparison with the known versions, and more especially with Jerome's, that we have here a really genuine, independent and thus very important version ; and not merely a translation or slight adaptation of one of the known versions. For to state it briefly, we have here, if not the very original of Jerome's text, at least a version which comes nearer to that ancient version than any other, and may be the old original. All the peculiar incidents which distinguish that text occur also in this Hebrew version. The similarity is so great, that at the first glance, one appears to be the direct translation of the other. On more minute examination we find, however, a number of variants, great and important enough to secure the independence of the Hebrew from the Latin, but not so easily *vice versâ.* The Hebrew text is in some parts more enlarged, and in others shorter than Jerome. It is characteristic that both the dog and every mention of Aqiqar as well as of Nadan or Laban is missing in H.L. The latter part of the XIIIth and of the XIVth chapter are also wanting. The prayers are mostly different, and greatly resemble the prayers of the Hebrew liturgy. The language is modelled after that of the Bible, the phraseology of which is closely imitated, and is, in skill and expression, vastly superior to that of H.M. and H F., both of which betray the influence of the rabbinical terminology. The author of H.L. had the Bible at his fingers' ends. At the same time, there occur at least two direct parallels to formulas of the liturgy (VIII, 5, 6 ; XIII, 11), and numerous other reminiscences. But as these were known already in the time of the Talmud and probably in that of the Mishna, they are of comparatively great antiquity. A few might be interpolations made by the first copyist. The language seems in some passages rather forced and somewhat artificial.

And yet by a close examination we convince ourselves that it is to a great extent the language of the prayers formulated at the time of the Second Temple, and what is more important, that this peculiar form of biblical and postbiblical language is shared by the recently discovered fragments of Ecclesiasticus and also of other Hebrew apocryphal texts such as the Testament of Naftali and the History of Judith in the version to which I have referred above. This language resembles more that of the last writers in the Bible, such as Ezra and Nehemia, as well as Daniel, in spite of the frequent use of other more archaic forms borrowed from older texts. There are also a few peculiarities, which I point out at the end of this publication, that show the transition from the language of the Bible to the so-called New-Hebrew. We may therefore safely see in this text the *oldest reflex* of the very *original* from which all the rest has flown. That it should have been translated at a very early period into the vernacular (Aramaic) is not at all surprising, and being excluded from the Canon, the Hebrew original soon disappeared. For this reason Jerome speaks only of the Aramaic, which must henceforth be considered as one of the versions and not as the original.

One can also not easily set aside the argument of Prof. Graetz (*Monatschrift*, 1879 p. 145 ff.), according to which the " Aramaic " of Jerome may mean the Hebrew language of the postbiblical time in distinction of that of the Bible. Jerome had no name for this development of Hebrew, and as some Aramaic words had been admitted into this language, not having a better to designate it, he called it pure and simple Aramaic. Graetz has pointed out many mistakes in the Greek and Latin translations, which can only be explained as misunderstandings of a purely Hebrew text. True, against this view stand the explicit words of Jerome, that the original of Tobit had to be translated to him into Hebrew. The language of this newly discovered text is, however, so much akin to bibilical Hebrew, that if we believe this to have been the source of Jerome, it is somewhat difficult to explain the necessity for another translator. Jerome could have easily mastered the text without any further assistance from a Jew. But he may have had the Aramaic version of this text.

If H.L. should be a translation from another language, and in this case Aramaic is the nearest to be thought of, then the translator has disguised his dependence upon another text so skilfully that it cannot be detected. The deep-going differences from the Greek versions exclude these from our purview, and the frequent discrepancies between this text and Jerome's, make it equally impossible to look upon the latter as a possible source from which the Hebrew might have been translated. There are so many obscure passages in the Latin and Greek versions which are now satisfactorily explained through this text, that they warrant the assumption that we have in our text, thus far, not a translation, but the oldest and best Semitic form of that original, from which Jerome made his translation, and to which B.C. refer, though indirectly. Quite peculiar to this text is the fact, that the author introduces the three friends of Job, who come and speak to Tobit, in the same manner in which they spoke to Job. The author must have thought these two to have been contemporaries, both living in the time of the first Assyrian conquest of Palestine. He alone avoids the confusion between the various forms of tithes, so conspicuous in all the other versions. He alone gives a correct reason for the sleeping of Tobit outside the house and being blinded by it. There is no trace of the agnate-marriage of which so much has been made by Rosenmann* and others. The men die in the first night only because they are not those who were appointed by God to be wedded to Sarah. We find here the explanation of the mysterious passage in Jerome (vi, 20 = Hebrew vi, 15), " In the second night thou shalt be admitted in the society of the holy patriarchs." The Hebrew has, " on the first night, remember the name of the holy patriarchs," which is in strict accordance with the Hebrew formulas of prayers, in which mention in the first instance is made of the names of the patriarchs, and their intercession is invoked on behalf of the one who prays to obtain grace from God. The prayers uttered by Tobit and Sarah are the outcome of that very injunction. Both appeal to the history of the patriarchs, and add : as God had heard their prayers, so may He listen to the prayers of these two youths. An ancient analogy is to be found in the liturgy of the fast day as prescribed in the Mishna (Taanith, ch. ii). There are besides other numerous analogies to the forms of the ancient Hebrew liturgy in this version

* Studien zum Buche Tobit : Berlin, 1894.

of Tobit, which if they are due to the author, and are not later interpolations and amplifications, might assist to fix the date of this composition. As far as I have been able to ascertain, all these allusions and parallels are found also in the Talmud, and in those prayers which form the basis of the Hebrew service, and are not later than the last century before the common era. The author knows, however, also the conclusion of the Amidah (the "Acathiston" of the Greek Church), to be Ps. xix, v. 15 (viii, 12), which may be much older than it has hitherto been assumed. The formula of betrothal (iii, 5–7) is more archaic than that of the actual liturgy, and on the other hand there is a poem connected with it (V. 8) which is an alphabtetical acrostic, and has been retained in a fragmentary form in the German liturgy. As it resembles similar hymns in the Hechaloth of R. Ishmael, it may also be very old. These indications do not allow us to see in our text a modern compilation or a translation made in comparatively recent times. It reflects much more the time when the liturgy had not yet been fixed, and much latitude was given to the individual. The form of these hymns and praises remind one of those in the book of Judith, the Song of the Three Children, and the so called Psalms of Solomon, all belonging to the first century before the common era.

Minor differences between this text and Jerome's, as this alone can truly be compared with it, I need not mention here. They are apparent to every one who reads the translation with the variations from Jerome which I have added thereunto.

The MS., as I remarked above, is very calligraphically written and with some care. The original must however not have been very correct, as in many instances there are evident lacunæ and other mistakes, with which I should not like to charge the copyist, as he seems to have done his work with care and circumspection, noting what he believed to be a mistake, and omitting to write those letters which he probably could not decipher.

In publishing this text I have reproduced it exactly as it stands in the MS., and in footnotes I have, in the first instance, indicated the biblical passages which the writer or translator had used in his work ; I have also referred to the passages in the Talmud which present analogies to the liturgical portions, and I have inserted in brackets in the text itself all the corrections and emendations.

Looking now upon our newly-recovered Hebrew text in the light which I have tried to throw upon it, we may confidently assert that we have here undoubtedly the oldest Semitic text extant—older than Jerome and Vetus Latin, and coming nearest to the lost Hebrew original, if it does not faithfully represent it. I am not prepared to state dogmatically the relation in which this text stands to the Greek, be it the B-C or be it the A version. It is evident from the comparison that B-C comes nearer to our text, but there are so many points of difference even between B-C and H.L. that it is exceedingly difficult to say with any certainty whether B-C depends on H.L. or is independent of it. There are also a few points of contact between H.L. and A, although more scarce.

In apportioning the right place to H.L. in the history of the texts, we are guided by the same considerations which must have guided Jerome when he made his translation. He preferred the text, which was almost identical with H.L., to the Greek. He must have believed, if he had not known it for a fact, that that was the original, while the Greek, in whatever recension, was an adaptation and a revision of that Semitic text. If that be the case, and I am inclined to believe it, then H.L. will be the oldest and best text, and of the Greek, B-C will represent the older version, as Reusch and others thought, and not A, as has been asserted by Fritzsche, Noeldeke, Schuerer, and others.

I publish together with the Hebrew text an English translation and a few notes. In order to facilitate research I have divided it into chapters, following the division of the Greek version, and have numbered the verses according to the division I found in the MS. I have also added the numbers of the verses according to A and to Jerome's division. As H.L. stands in the closest connection with Jerome's text, I print in square brackets [] those portions wherein. H.L. differs from Jerome's text, and add in footnotes the variations and the verses from Jerome missing in our text. The numbers of verses as added in round brackets are those of Jerome's version.

I pass now to the study of the other text, no less interesting than the last, but from another point of view. Whilst H.L. furnished us a link upwards, this here furnishes a link downwards in the history of the transmission of the text in the later literature. Dr. Neubauer published together with the Aramaic text a peculiar legend from the Midraš Tanḥuma, the first half of which contains a parallel to the incident of Sara and her seven husbands who died, whilst Tobit withstood successfully the attack of the demon, whose place is taken in this legend by the angel of death. The second half

belongs to a different cycle of legends of which the oldest and most
complete version is found in my MS. No. 82, fol. 100*a*, No. 130
(cf. Jellinek, *Beth-hamidrasch* V, 152–154 and I, p. 83–84).   That
legend was added to the Tanḥuma by the editor of the Mantua
edition, who indicates as his source the same work as that given for
the Aramaic version of Dr. Neubauer, viz., the Midrash Rabba of
R. Moses had Darshan (the Preacher).   The connection between
these two versions is however very slender.   There are many intermediary links missing, which should explain the gradual shrinking
of the elaborate tale to a small legend.   Joseph Zabara, who lived
about the year 1200, and who wrote his " Book of Delight " in
Barcelona, or Narbonne, introduces among other tales a peculiar
version of the Tobit-legend (translated into English along with the
other tales by Mr. I. Abrahams, in *The Jewish Quarterly Review*, VI,
1894, pp. 522–524).   This version, reprinted by Hugin in
מעשים טובים   Bagdad, 1890, fol. 6*a*–8*b*, is almost a perversion of
the legend.   The only point of interest is that only three persons are
mentioned in connection with Sara instead of seven, and in this
number the Tanḥuma agrees with Zabara.   Not from this source
however did the legend come into the Midrash, but, as we have
seen, from the Midrash of Moses the preacher.   I have discovered now
the exact counterpart in Hebrew to the Aramaic text of Dr. Neubauer,
and what is more, have found it also in a collection of homiletic
interpretations of the Pentateuch.   The MS. is private property,
and I was allowed many years ago to take a complete copy of this
Midrash.   It was then already half deteriorated by age and damp-
ness and portions of the leaves were crumbling away at the slightest
touch.   I have reason to believe that we may consider the original
MS. as lost since.   Happily I have a complete copy of the whole work.
The original was written in a Spanish hand, and belonged in all
probability to the 15th century, if not earlier.   The character of this
Midrash is very much like that published by Buber in 1894 under the
title "Agadischer Commentar zum Pentateuch."   My MS. (I may now
call it my MS., the other being as good as lost) seems to represent
an older and more complete text, as it also contains homilies to
the Haphtaroth and to the various festivals, which are not to be
found in that edited by Buber.   In the contents there are also
marked differences, but still both texts belong to one and the same
group, having many points in common.   In this MS. (Codex Or.
Gaster 28), we find a homily for the second day of Pentecost,

the first part of which is a literal translation of the Aramaic text, but very much shortened towards the end. The greatest stress is laid on the giving of tithes, and the history of Tobit is adduced as an example of the grace of God bestowed on the man who fulfils faithfully the duty of paying his tithes. The lesson for the second day of Pentecost commences with the verse, Deut. xiv, 22, " Thou shalt surely tithe all the increase of thy seed, that which cometh forth of the field year by year." The same words stand at the head of the Aramaic text and of the Hebrew. Here the introduction is more spun out than in the Aramaic text, which is merely an abridged copy of the original. Through this official connection with the liturgy one understands the reason why in the Aramaic and in this Hebrew version, which I will call H.G. (Hebrew Gaster), and in Ar. mention is made (II, 1) of the feast of Pentecost. Jerome and H.L. have merely a *feast of the Lord*. It may just as well be, that because this feast is mentioned in the legend the legend itself was brought in connection with the lesson of that day.

Now H.G. follows Aramaic as closely as possible, though leaving out the greater part of the legend ; all the minor incidents and almost all the prayers are missing, so that the whole book is reduced to a comparatively short tale. But whatever there is left, is a literal translation which sometimes forces the character of the Hebrew. Thus it proves also the fact that Aramaic texts were translated into Hebrew at a later period, and that the legend of Tobit enjoyed a great reputation, and was preserved mainly through its connection with the liturgy. H.L. is also included in a volume containing all those books and poems which are usually associated with the prayer-book and synagogue service. Through this connection one understands the reason for its continual dwindling in size. It served as an illustration of the teaching of the Law, and was treated as such.

By comparing H.G. with the Aramaic, we shall find that among other things omitted in both is that peculiar legend of the intended sacrifice of the two sons of Sennacherib, mentioned in H.M., chapter I. But the very same legend occurs in my MS. (28) in the homily preceding that of the Tobit legend. We have thus an indication of the probable source of this version (H.M.). It was in every probability taken from this or a very similar collection of homilies.

The minute comparison of the Aramaic (Neub.) with H.G. (for which that is the direct original), besides being interesting as illustrating the way how the abridgement was effected, is also of value for critical purposes. One point is especially important. When Tobi deposits the money with Gabael he received from him, according to the Greek, *a handwriting* (v, 3) or a *note of hand*, so also Itala and Jer. H.L. has, *a token* (iv, 10), Ar. and H.M. have instead *a bag*, which to say the least, is very incongruous. In H.G. we have *a ring* as a token, which seems to be superior to all the rest. With a slight alteration one could amend the word אמתחת, *bag*, of H.M., into חתמת, which means a *seal*. This would imply that the Aramaic is a translation from the corrupted Hebrew text and not *vice versâ*. But one example alone would not suffice to determine definitely the position in which those texts stand to one another. Without pursuing, therefore, this question any further, I limit myself merely to pointing it out. Many other similar contributions to the criticism of the text are to be found in this Hebrew version, for which reason I publish this also, and add an English translation to it. I have divided it into chapters according to the Aramaic and Greek, but without the division of verses, as these chapters are very small, and it is quite unnecessary to subdivide them any further.

In order to be as complete as possible, I will mention in conclusion another text of the Tobit legend, which although printed, has, so far as I have been able to ascertain, escaped the notice of every bibliographer, nor have I been able to find another copy in any library but my own. In 1851 there appeared in Lemberg a book called Oṣar Haqqodesh, which gives itself out to be a reprint of an older Amsterdam edition. I have not been able to trace it. Perhaps some one else will be more fortunate in that respect. Now this little book contains, in the first place, our Tobit legend in a very shortened form. The text is divided into twelve chapters, and agrees in the main, as far as the plot is concerned, with A., but not absolutely. Without being a literal translation, it is a more faithful reflex of A than H.F. A few incidents are worth noticing, such as the correct Hebrew name Ahmata for Egbatanis; the proper translation of the name of the river, as Hideqel instead of Tigris, though Rage is spelt Ragez, and Raguel instead of Reuel. In one point, this text agrees with H.L. alone, where all the other versions differ. When Sara prays in the anguish of her soul, she says in H.L., "I know that thou (oh God) hast appointed the right man to be my husband, and if it be Thy will, send him to me."

In Jerome we have a faint trace of it. Sara says (in III, 19), "because, perhaps thou hast kept me for another man." In this printed edition we find that she almost expects her relative to be her husband but he would certainly shrink from marrying a woman who would thereby cause his death, and she prays either to be healed or rather to die. Nothing of this is to be found in the Greek ; there are also a few other incidents similarly independent of the Greek. I must limit myself merely to point these out and to draw the attention of scholars to the vast material in Hebrew literature which has hitherto not been utilised for a thorough study of the Apocrypha.

II.—TRANSLATION.

Tobit Legend I (H.L.).

I. **1** (1)* The words of Tobi, son of Tobiel, son of Hananel, the son of Asael, the son of Gabatiel of the tribe of Nephtali in Galil, on (the river) Pishon, behind the way of the going down of the sun on the left side ; and the name of the town was Safet. **2** (2) And Tobi was made captive and exiled in the days of Shalmanasar, king of Assur. (3) Even in his captivity he forsook not the way of truth, and whatever he got he gave in equal parts to his brethren the captives. (4) And he was the servant to the whole tribe of Nephtali, and he did not pull away the shoulder from the work. **3** (5) And when Israel was dwelling in his land he went astray and worshipped the golden calves, which Jeroboam, the son of Nebat, had made ; (6) but that man Tobi used to go and bring sacrifices in the house of the Lord, and adored there the God of Israel. **4** (7) And all the first-fruits of his land and his tithes he brought faithfully into the house of God even unto his temple in the third year, the year of tithes ; (8) and from his youth he kept the ways of the Lord and his commandments. **5** (9) And when Tobi grew to be a man, he took a wife from his tribe, by name Anna ; and she was with child and bare a son ; and she called his name Tobiyah. **6** (10) And Tobi poured out his heart over him, and taught him the

---

* The numbers in round brackets are the verses according to Jerome and LXX ; and the passages in square brackets [] are missing in or differing from Jerome's version.

ways of the Lord. And he walked in the ways of his father and abstained from all sin. 7 (11) And he and his wife and son came into the land of Assur, into Nineveh the great city, together with the whole tribe Nephtali. (12) And they all defiled themselves with the food of the Gentiles, but Tobi alone did not defile himself. 8 (13) And he served God with all his heart, and God gave him grace and favour before Shalmanassar, the king, (14) and he made him master over everything that he wished, and he gave him liberty to do whatever he wished in the whole kingdom. 9 (15) And he went into all the towns and fortresses to see the captivity, and to ask after and seek their welfare. 10 (16) And when he had come to Madai he had in his hand a large fortune, which the king had given to him, 1,000 talents of silver. (17) And he gathered a multitude of Jews from his tribe, and he entrusted the silver to Gabiel, and they saw it and were witnesses, and he gave him a token in remembrance of the money. 11 (18) After a long time Shalmanassar, the king of Assur, died, and his son Sennacherib reigned after him, and the children of Israel were evily treated. 12 (19) And Tobi distributed his goods and gave it to his kindred and comforted them. 13 And he gave to every one as he was able. (20) He clothed the naked and fed the hungry, and the dead that were slain he buried. 14 (21) And when Sennacherib had come back from the land of Judah with ignominy by reason of the slaughter that God had made about him because he had blasphemed and slandered, that Sennacherib having been humbled, slew many of the Israelites, and Tobi used to bury them. 15 (22) And it was told the king, and he commanded him to be slain, and all his substance to be plundered. 16 (23) And Tobi fled with his wife and son, and they (wandered about) naked and barefooted in the frost without any covering and without sustenance; but wherever he went he found many friends. 17 (24) And it came to pass that after forty-five days the sons of Sennacherib, Essarhaddon and Sharezer, killed him, (25) and Tobi hearing of it, returned to his home, and all his substance was restored to him.

II. 1 (1) And it was after this there was a festival of the Lord, and Tobi prepared a great dinner in his house. 2 (2) And he said to his son Tobiyah: go and bring some of our tribe that fear God to feast with us. 3 (3) And Tobiyah went and returned and told his father that he had seen one of the children of Israel slain lying in the street. 4 And Tobi got up from his seat and left the dinner; he ate nothing, (4) but went to the body, took it up and carried it privately to his house, and when the sun went down he buried it,* (5) and ate afterwards with mourning and fear. **5** (6) And he remembered the word spoken through Amos the prophet, and I will turn your feasts into mourning and your songs into lamentation.† **6** (8) And his relations blamed him, saying : Thou knowest well that the king had given out a command to slay thee because thou didst bury the dead, and thou didst flee and savedst thyself by it, and yet thou still holdest fast thine integrity. **7** (9) And he said : I fear the Lord of Lords more than the king, who is, like me, formed also of clay. **8** And Tobi continued to go after the slain, and he used to bring them secretly into his house and bury them at midnight. **9** (10) Now it happened one day that Tobi was wearied with burying them, [and he had not washed his hands nor cleansed them in water after the burial of them.] **10** And he cast himself down on a bed by the wall and slept, (11) and there was the nest of small birds (swallows or sparrows), and their dung fell upon his eyes and his eyes were dim so that he could not see. (12) And God did this to him in order to try him as he had done to Job. **11** (13) And whereas Tobi feared God from his infancy, he did not for all this charge God with foolishness, (14) and he clung to the God of Israel and trusted in his mercy. **12** (15) And the friends of Job, Eliphaz the Temanite, and Bildad the Shuhite, and Zophar the Naamathite came to him, and they all mocked at him saying : (16) where is thy righteousness upon which thou trustest, saying, I am just and I will bury the dead and bestow mercy upon them? (17) And Tobi rebuked them and said : (18) truly [I am clean and I am innocent, and my righteousness will answer for me, and we must receive the evil as well as the good with love and gladness of heart, for all the judgments of God are right]. **14** For everyone whose faith is perfect will not change nor alter,‡ and God gives him the life of the world to come. **15** (19) And his wife was wise hearted to work in all manner of cunning workmanship, and she worked for many and she fed her husband by the work of her hands. **16** (20) Whereby it came to pass that every (l. one) day she received a young kid for her wages and she brought it home. [And the kid went through the house bleating.] **17** (21) And Tobi heard

* J. reads : That after the sun was down he might bury him.
† J. 7 omitted here.
‡ J. 18 reads instead : For we are the children of saints and look for that life which God will give to those that never change their faith from Him.

B

the voice of the kid and he said to her: take heed lest perhaps it be stolen, restore it to its owners, for thus are we commanded by our God, and it is not lawful for us to keep it over night in our house or to take it to ourselves.   **18** (22) And she answered and said: if thou art righteous as thou sayest, wherefore has all this trouble come upon thee?   Such was her custom to speak every day roughly with him [until he was wearied of his life].

III. **1** (1) And when Tobi heard [all these rebukes] he sighed and was sorely grieved, and he turned his face towards the wall, and he prayed with tears: (2) And he said: thou art just, O Lord, and thy judgments right and thy ways are mercy and loving kindness and truth and judgment.   **2** (3) And now, O Lord, remember me [for good and visit me with thy salvation], and do not remember the sins [of my parents], and hear me quickly, and the offences of my forefathers do not remember against me.   **3** (4) For because we have not observed thy commandments, therefore have we been made to be a fable and a reproach among all the nations whither thou hast brought us.   **4** (5) And now, O Lord, great are thy works,* (6) and thou doest what is right in thy sight.   And thou, O perfect Rock, do with me according to thy mercy, love, and truth, and take my soul; for it is better for me to die, than to live.   **5** (7) The same time it came to pass that Sarah, the daughter of Reuel, brother of Tobi [was praying to God], in Madai.   **6** [For] she had heard reproaches [and contempts and she was despised in the eyes] of one of her father's servants.   **7** (8) and she provoked her sore every day saying: woe unto thee and to thy luck, for seven men were given unto thee, and they died every one of them the very first night they went in to thee, through thy witchcraft.†   **8** And how darest thou to lift up thine eyes and to raise thy head to speak to me on either a great or a small thing, as I am better than thou.   **9** But this was an untruth in her mouth, as it was through no fault of hers, as Ashmedai the king of the demons killed them on the first night, because she was not appointed for them.   **10** (9) And every day she used to say to her: lo, thou art unworthy of a husband or to have seed upon the earth, and (10) now thou thinkest to kill me as thou hast killed them.   **11** And it came to pass one day that she went up into the upper

---

* J. reads: "Great are thy judgments, because we have not done according to thy precepts, and have not walked sincerely before thee."

† (8) different in J.   (8) Because she had been given to seven husbands, and a devil named Asmodeus had killed them at their first going in unto her.

)om and stayed there three days, night and day, she neither ate
read nor drank any water (11) and stood in prayers and supplication
before God that he would avenge her [on that servant] who upbraided
er. **12** [And she thought to have killed herself if she had not been
afraid that she would bring down the gray hairs of her father in
sorrow to the grave and that their enemies should not say in
derision : " he had one single daughter and she has killed herself"].
3 (12) And when the three days had come to an end she fell down
and prayed to God, saying : **14** (13) Blessed art thou, O Lord God of
Israel, who keepeth his covenant and mercy with them that observe
his covenant and love his commandments. **15** Thou answerest in
time of tribulation, thou deliverest, rescuest, and savest and bestowest
benefits on the guilty. **16** (14) To thee I lift up my eyes, to thee,
who dwellest in the heavens [for I know that I am dust and to dust
I shall return]. **17** (15) To thee I pray now, and before thee I
present my supplication with regard to those who reproached me
undeservedly.* **18** (16) Thou knowest my heart, that I never coveted
a husband, and I am standing pure before thee. **19** (17) I did not
sit in the seat of the scornful, nor have I joined myself with them
that play, nor did I walk with the wicked. (18) I would not have
desired to take a husband, were it not for my reverence for thee†
(19) nor was I appointed for them. **20** I know that thou hast kept (?)
and appointed another man for me‡ (20) [and if it be thy will, send
him to me], (21) for such is the law of the man who worshippeth
thee in truth, that his end is hope. **21** And when tribulation and
anxiety comes upon him thou deliverest him through thy mercy,
(22) for thou art not delighted§ in the death of him that dieth, but
that he return from his way and live, for piety averts the evil decree.
22 (23). Be thy name blessed for ever and ever. Amen! (24) At
that time her cry and that of Tobi were heard as they prayed
together, and their cry went up before God. (25) And he sent
his angel Raphael to heal them and to deliver them from their
tribulation.

* J. reads : I beg, O Lord, that thou loose me from the bond of this reproach,
or else take me away from the earth.

† J. reads : But a husband I consented to take, with thy fear, not with my
lust.

‡ J. reads : And either I was unworthy of them, or they perhaps were not
worthy of me : because perhaps thou hast kept me for another man.

§ J. continues :—in our being lost ; because after a storm thou makest a calm,
and after tears and weaping thou pourest in joyfulness.

IV. **1** (1) *And Tobi was praying for his death, and he called his son Tobiyah, (2) and said ֻ **2** My son, hear the instruction of thy father, and forsake not the teaching of thy mother, and bind their instruction upon thine heart. **3** (3) When God shall take my soul, thou shalt take me and bury me after the burial of my fathers, and thou shalt honour thy mother all the days of thy life. **4** (4) And thou shalt be mindful of the tribulations which have come upon us and upon her every day; (5) and when she will have fulfilled the days of her life, bury her with honour by me. **5** (6) And thou shalt be mindful of thy Creator all the days of thy life, and take heed never to sin, and keep the commandments of thy God and his law. **6** (7) Thou shalt surely open thine hand to the poor [when thou seest the naked, do thou cover him. **7** Deal thy bread to the hungry]† and hide not thine eyes from them, then God will bless thee in all the work of thy hands, (10) and he will open unto thee his good treasure, (11) for riches profit not in the day of wrath, but righteousness delivereth from death. **8** (12–14) And fear God with all thy heart and all thy might; do not join thyself with evil-doers and do not sit in the seat of the scoffers. **9** (15) Render to every man according to his work, and give him his wages on the very day, and let not the wages of the hired servant tarry with thee. (16) Love thy neighbour as thyself, (17 and 19)‡ and seek the counsel of the pious. **10** (21) And now, my son, go and ask for the talents of silver which I have left in the hand of Gabiel, in the city of Dago (Rage). (22) And here is the token which I have given him in memory of the money. (23) Fear not, for God will be with thee wherever thou goest, if thou keepest his commandments. **11** [Be not dismayed on account of the great tribulations which have befallen us, for I trust, through the fear of God, that we shall still have great salvation and deliverance, my son; fear not.]

1 V. (1) Then Tobiyah answered his father and said: I will do all the things which thou hast commanded me, (2) but teach me

---

* J. reads:—Therefore when Tobias thought that his prayer was heard that he might die he called, etc.

† (8 and 9 of J. missing here. (8) According to thy ability be merciful. (9) If thou have much, give abundantly: if thou have little, take care even so to bestow willingly a little.

‡ (J. 18 and 20) missing here. (18) Lay out thy bread and thy wine upon the burial of a just man, and do not eat and drink thereof with the wicked. (20) Bless God at all times, and desire of him to direct thy ways, and that all thy counsels may abide in him.

and show me the way I should go, for I am only one, and how can
I go alone to bring the money? **2** (4) And he said: go outside
and seek thee out some faithful man that I should give him his hire
while I yet live [and he will go with thee to get the money].
3 (5) And Tobiyah went out that very day, and went [into the market-
places of the town to seek a faithful man. **4** And the angel Raphael
went out to meet him—he was sent by God to assist him]† (6) and
the lad knew not that he was an angel. **5** And the lad saluted him
and he asked him: who art thou, my lord? (7) And he said: I
am of the children of Judah. **6** And Tobiyah said: knowest thou
the way that leadeth to Naphtali? (8) And he answered and said:
I know all the boundaries of the lands and countries, **7** and I know
Gabael, our kinsman, who lives in the city of Dage (Rage), in Madai,
in the city of Nineveh, on the mount Abtanim (C. Egbatanis).
8 (9) And Tobiyah said: let not my lord be angry, I will only go
to my father and return. **9** (10) And Tobiyah went and told his
father,‡ and Tobi sent for the man. And (11) he came to Tobi and
saluted him. **10** And the angel said: gladness and joy mayest thou
obtain! **11** (12) And he said to him: What manner of joy can there
be to me who sit in darkness [like the dead] and cannot see any
more the light of the sun? **12** (13)§ And he said: let it not be
grievous in thy sight, for thy salvation is near at hand; thou wilt see
again and thy heart will rejoice, **13** (14) And Tobi said to him: I
have called thee to go with my son (to) Gabael, who dwelleth in Dage
(Rage) in the country of Madai, and when thou shalt return I will
pay thee thy hire.

  14 (15) And the angel said: Here I am, ready to go with him.
(16) And Tobit said to him: Tell me what is thy name, and of what
family and what tribe art thou? **16** (17, 18) And the angel answered
and said: My name is Azaryah, son of the great (elder) Hananyah.‖

  * (J. 3) omitted here. (3) Then his father answered him and said: I have
a note of his hand with me, which thou shalt show him, he will presently pay it.

  † J. reads: Then Tobias going forth found a beautiful young man, standing
girded, and as it were ready to walk.

  ‡ J. adds: Upon which, his father being in admiration, desired that he would
come in unto him.

  § Different in J. (13) And the young man said to him: Be of good
courage, thy cure from God is at hand.

  ‖ (J. 17–18) Different. (17) And Raphael, the angel, answered: Dost thou
seek the family of him thou hirest or the hired servant himself to go with thy
son? (18) But lest I should make thee uneasy, I am Azarias the son of the great
Ananias.

I am descended from a noble family. **17** (19) And Tobi said : let it not be grievous in thy sight (do not be angry, I pray thee), and tell me of what family art thou ? And he answered : I am from the tribe . . . . .* (21) And Tobi said : may God be with you and send his angel before you. (22) **And they prepared provisions for the journey, and they set out together. 18** (23-25)† And Anna his mother went with him until the outskirts of the town, weeping all the way she went. **19.** [And she said to them : May God be with you and give you grace and mercy in the eyes of the inhabitants of the land. **20** And now let thy footsteps be apace to return quickly to us, before we die and go down in sorrow to the grave. **21** And when she returned home] she said to Tobi : what hast thou done that thou hast sent away from thee [thine only son whom thou lovest? **22** If mischief befal him, then shall we bring down our grey hairs with sorrow to the grave. **23** For as long as our son was with us, he was to us] (as one who refreshes our soul and) a restorer of life and a nourisher of our old age. **24** (26) And he answered her : Fear not, my sister,‡ (27) for God has sent his angel with him, and he will make his way prosperous for him, and he shall restore him yet to us.§

VI. **1** (1) And Tobiyah went, and came to the River Hideqel (Tigris), and he stayed there. (2) And he went down to wash his feet, and behold a great fish suddenly leaped out, and would have swallowed (devoured) him, (3) and he was afraid, and cried out with a loud voice, and said : My Lord,|| save me from this great fish.¶ **2** (5) And the angel said to him : open it and take out its heart, gall, and liver, and lay them out safely, for they will serve thee as

---

* J. (20) Omitted here : and the angel said to him, I will lead thy son safe and bring him to thee again safe.

† J. (23-25) Different. (23) And when they were departed, his mother began to weep, and to say : Thou hast taken the staff of our age, and sent him away from us. (24) I wish the money for which thou hast sent him, had never been. (25) For our poverty was sufficient for us, that we might account it as riches that we saw our son.

‡ Jer. adds : our son will arrive thither safe and will return safe to us and thy eyes shall see him.

§ J. (28) omitted here, "at these words his mother ceased weeping and held her peace."

|| Diff. in J : My Lord (Sir), he cometh upon me.

¶ J. (4) omitted here. (4) And the angel said to him, take him by the gill, and draw him to thee. And when he had done so, he drew him out upon the land, and he began to pant before his feet.

medicine. **3** (6) And he took hold of the fish and divided it in the midst, and they ate one half, and the other they made into provisions for the journey, till they came to Dage (Rage) in the land of Madai. **4** (7) And the lad asked the angel, to what use is the heart and the liver and the gall which we have put up safely? **5** (8) And he answered and said: take the heart to drive away evil spirits from man or woman, if you burn it on fire.* **6** (10) And the lad asked him: where shall we lodge to-night? (11) And he said: [in the city of Rage]. **7** Behold [in this town] there is a good man whose name is Reuel, of thy father's family, and he has neither son nor daughter but one single daughter,† (12) and she inherits all the substance of her father, (13) and when you come there, ask her father for her, for he will not withhold her from thee. **8** (14) And Tobiyah answered and said: [hear me, and so may God hear thee!] **9** [I have heard, and my belly trembled.] I heard [from many who uttered slander] that she had been given in marriage to seven husbands, and the first night on their going in to her, Ashmedai, king of the evil spirits, came in the middle of the night and killed them. **10** (15) Therefore I hold back, and am afraid lest (the same thing should happen to me) as to one of them. I am young, and an only son to my father and mother, and if the same thing should happen to me, I should bring down their gray hairs with blood to the grave. **11** (16) And the angel said to him: be not affrighted nor be thou dismayed, nor let thy heart faint, for I will show thee how to drive him away from thee. **12** (17) Know that all these men who were killed were not suited (or fit) for her that any seed should come from them, therefore has the demon killed them.‡ **13** (18) But thou shalt do what I command thee: be together with her in one chamber three days and three nights, and do not approach her.§ **14** (19) And every night thou shalt burn the liver on the fire [and fumigate the bed on which you will lie], and the demon will fly away. **15** (20) On the first night,

---

* J. (9) omitted here. (9) And the gall is good for anointing the eyes in which there is a white speck, and they shall be cured.

† (12 and 13) somewhat different in J.

‡ (17) Diff. in J. : For they who in such manner receive matrimony as to shut out God from themselves and from their mind, and to give themselves to their lust, as the horse and mule, which have no understanding, over them the devil hath power.

§ J. adds : And give thyself to nothing else but to prayers with her.

remember the names of the holy patriarchs,* (21) on the second,
pray to God that good men may come from you.† **16** (22) And on
the third night, about the time of the cock-crowing, do thy will with
the fear of the Lord, and he will bless thee.‡

VII. **1** (1) And they went into the house of Reuel, and he
rejoiced very much, (2) and he kissed Tobiyah, and said to his wife
Ednah: behold how like he is to the good man Tobi. **2** (3) And
she [his wife] said: who are ye, and whence do you come? (4) And
he said: from the land of Naphtali, of the captivity in Nineveh.
3 (5) And Reuel said to them: do you know my brother Tobi?
[And the angel said:] we know him (6),§ and this young man is
his son, and his name is Tobiyah. **4** (7) And Reuel went and fell
upon his face and kissed him and wept upon his neck. **5** And he
said: blessed be thou of the Lord, for thou art the son of a good
man. (8) And they came, Ednah his wife (and his daughter), and
they wept over him. (9) And they prepared a feast, and they killed
a young goat and sat down to dinner. **6** (10) And Tobiyah said:
Uncle! [I ask a great request of thee; I pray thee, my lord, deny
me not.]‖ **7** Consent now to give me thy daughter for a wife [it is
better that you should give her to me, than that you should give her
to another man, as I am thy flesh and thy bone.] **8** (11) And
Reuel was terrified, and he was afraid lest he should die as those
men died through her, and he kept his mouth with a bridle.
9 (12) And the angel said: be not afraid, as fortune has come,
and in the name of God, give her to him, for the others were not
appointed unto her, and this one is appointed. **10** (13)¶ And
Reuel answered: oh, would that it were as thou sayest!** [may

* J. (20): But the second night thou shalt be admitted into the society
of the holy patriarchs.

† J. (21) On the third night thou shalt obtain a blessing, that sound children
may be born of you.

‡ J. (22) And when the third night is past, thou shalt take the virgin with the
fear of the Lord, moved rather for love of children than for lust, that in the seed of
Abraham thou mayest obtain a blessing in children.

§ J. (6) reads: And when he was speaking many good things of him, the angel
said to Raguel, Tobias, concerning whom thou inquirest, is this young man's father.

‖ J. adds, I will not eat nor drink this day unless thou, etc.

¶ J. (13) reads, I doubt not but God hath regarded my prayers and tears in
his sight.

** J. (14) omitted:—And I believe he hath therefore made you come to me,
that this maid might be married to one of her own kindred according to the
law of Moses; and now doubt not, but I will give her to thee!

the Lord God of Israel make their house to be like the house of Perez, and fulfil the wishes of their heart and their desire for good] (15) and the God of our fathers Abraham, Isaac, and Jacob be with them and command his blessing upon both of you. **11** (16) And the elders of the town gathered themselves together there, and they wrote the things down, (17) and they blessed God, the bridegroom, and the bride, and they ate and made merry.

I VIII. (1) And it came to pass after that, that they went both into the inner chamber. **2** (2) And Tobiyah remembered the words of the angel, and he took the liver and laid it upon burning coals, and the smoke thereof ascended. (3) And the angel took the demon and bound him and sent him into the desert which is before Egypt. **3** (4) And Tobiyah said to Sarah: arise, and let us pray to God to-night, and the following night, and on the third night we shall be in wedlock. (5) For we are children of saints, and we must not walk in the statutes of the nations that are round about us. **4** (6) So they both arose and prayed with reverence before God, [and they poured out their heart in prayer (supplication) before God]. **5** (7) *And Tobiyah said : blessed art thou, O Lord our God, king of the universe, who has created gladness and joy, bridegroom and bride. [**6** (8) Blessed art thou, O Lord, King of the universe, who has created man after thy own image and likeness, and who hast given him from the strength of thy power to know thee and to serve thee.] **7** Thou hast given him a helpmeet for him, and thou hast commanded them to be fruitful and to multiply their offspring in the midst of the land.† **8** [Lord over all, creator of all, mighty over all, who searches all, he is all powerful and exalted over all, all give song unto him, he establishes law and commandment for all, he is good to all, righteous and just to all, all powerful ; all give him praise, he sustains all, he answers all, he delivers all the captives, he is just and gracious to all, the Lord is nigh unto all, the Lord is merciful and his mercies are over all ; all give hymn unto him, his name supports all. **9** God of gods, and Lord of lords ! merciful has thy name been called from eternity ;

---

* J. (7 and 8) reads : And Tobias said, Lord God of our fathers, may the heavens and the earth, and the sea and the fountains, and the rivers, and all thy creatures that are in them, bless thee. (8) Thou madest Adam of the slime of the earth, and gavest him Eve for a helper.

† J. (7–10) correspond in our text to (**5–25**).

remember us according to thy loving kindness and mercy, for they
have been ever of old.   10 And remember for me the pious
acts of my father Tobi, who walked before thee in piety and truth ;
save me and rebuke the Satan so that he should not touch us
or hurt us.   11 Give me from this woman seed of men, that our
offspring may know thy name and study thy law, and it shall
be known among the nations that thou art the Lord and no other.
12 Then hear thou in heaven my prayer, as thou hast heard the
prayer of our holy fathers, the saints, the prayer of Abraham in
Ur Kasdim, and the prayer of Isaac on the Mount Moriah, and
the prayer of Jacob in Bethel, and the prayers of all the just ; and
put my tears into thy bottle. . Let the words of my mouth, and the
meditation of my heart be acceptable in thy sight, O Lord, my rock
and my redeemer.*   13 And Sarah prayed and said : The Lord, the
Lord is a god full of compassion, and gracious, slow to anger, and
abundant in mercy and truth ; keeping mercy for the thousands of
those who keep his laws and commandments.   14 O Lord, thou
alone art one, and there is no second beside thee ; who is like unto
thee, who can be likened unto thee, who can be compared with thee ?
there is no other save thee, and there is none beside thee, and there
is none to be equalled to thee.   15 Thou hast created everything,
and there is no forgetfulness before thee ; therefore the hearts
believe that thou art one, wondrous in all thy ways, hidden from
every eye and no eye can see thee.   Thou hast been before the
world came into existence, and after its destruction thou wilt be,
and thy years shall have no end.   16 Lo ! the host of heavens were
made by thy word, and thy hand was not in their creation ; thou
didst call them, and they all stood forth ; in thy hand is the power
and might to destroy them, and to change them and to restore them
to their original state.   17 In thy hand is life and good ; thou hast
created this world to try man by the statutes and judgments which
thou hast given to them.   And the world to come thou hast created
for thy pious men—those that love thee and keep thy covenant—
and hell thou hast prepared of old for the abominable and for those
who dealt treacherously with thee.   19 And thou art the Lord who
hast chosen the seed of Jeśurun from among all the nations which

---

* J. (9) reads instead : And now, O Lord, thou knowest not for fleshly lust do
I take my sister to wife, but only for the love of posterity, in which thy name
may be blessed for ever and ever

are upon the face of the earth, and hast performed (wrought) signs
and wonders in the face of all those who stood up against them.
20 And now, oh Lord, oh king, full of mercy, give ear to my prayer,
and hold not thy peace at my tears, as thou hast listened to the
prayer of our mother Sara ; when she prayed to thee because of her
handmaid Hagar, and to the prayer of Rebecca when the children
struggled together within her ; **21** and to the prayer of Rachel, the
mother of children, who was the barren woman in the house at the
time when her sister provoked her sore ; thou didst open her
womb, and she bare children that are standing in thy courts to serve
thee. **22** And the prayer of the prophetess Miriam, and the prayer of
the wife of Elqanah, when her rival provoked her sore, in order to
make her fret, thou appointedst a son from her to be a prophet,
to stand before thee and to minister unto thee, so may my prayer
ascend as a pleasure before thee, and may I be worthy of this man,
and send us of thy blessings. **23** And rebuke the Satan that he
should not touch my lord, and not stand at his right hand to be his
adversary. **24** Therefore we praise thee, O Lord our God, for all
thy miracles and numberless wonderful things, for heaven and the
heaven of heavens cannot contain thee, still less is man able to
investigate one of them. **25** Who can utter thy mighty acts, and
show forth all thy praises ; thou art exalted as head above all, and
extolled over all blessing.]*

26 (11) And it came to pass in the middle of the night, about the
cockcrowing, that Reuel cried to his servants : " Arise and dig quickly
a grave for Tobiyah, (12) for I know that mischief has befallen him
as it happened to the other seven men who made marriage with
us." **27** (13) And when they had finished digging the grave, Reuel
returned to the house, and said to his wife : (14) Send the maid
and let her see and ascertain whether the young man be dead or
alive.† **28** (15) And the maid went, and behold, both were alive,
lying in their bed and sleeping. (16) And she returned and brought
the good tidings, and their heart rejoiced. **29** (17) And they blessed
the Lord, and said : Blessed art thou, O Lord God of Israel, for
thou hast done well unto us, and thou hast wrought wonders (18),
and thou hast rebuked the Satan, so that he should not be able to

---

* Instead of vv. 13–25, J. reads : (10) Sarah also said, Have mercy on us,
O Lord, have mercy on us, and let us grow old both together in health.

† J. adds, that I may bury him before it be day.

harm us nor our children for ever, (19) and all the nations shall know that thy name is called upon us.* (20) And Reuel commanded them to fill up the pit from one end to another. **30** (21, 22) And he commanded, and they prepared a feast (slaughtered animals), and he called all his neighbours, and they ate and drank and made a great banquet.† **31** (23) And Reuel begged of Tobiyah to abide with him two weeks. **32** (24) And he gave him one half of his riches and substance, and treasures and his sheep, and his cattle and his oxen, and his household, and of whatever he possessed he would give (one half of) it to him in his lifetime, and after his death he would take it all.

IX. **1** (1, 2) And Tobiyah said to the angel : I beseech thee, my lord, let not thine anger burn against me, I have taken upon me to speak but this once, and do thou show more kindness in the latter end than at the beginning. **2** (3) And go for me to Gabael into the town (city) of . . . . and take these tokens into thy hands, and receive the silver from him, and invite him to come to the joy and to rejoice with us, (5?) as I cannot depart from here before the end of the two weeks, the days of the feast.‡ **3** (4) And thou knowest that my father will not rest nor be still until I return in peace. **4** (6) So the angel listened to him, and he took four of Reuel's servants and two camels with him, and came to Rage, and he gave the token to Gabael and took the silver from him. **5** (7) And he told what had happened to Tobiyah, the son of Tobi, and that he had asked him to come and rejoice with the invited on the day of his marriage, the day of the rejoicing of his heart. **6** [And Gabael arose and saddled his camel and went with him.] **7** (8) And when he had come into Reuel's house, he found him and Tobiyah with him, sitting at the table, and he fell upon his neck and kissed him and he wept. **8** (9) And he blessed him and said : The Lord bless thee and keep

---

* J. (18 and 19) reads : For thou hast shown thy mercy to us, and hast shut out from us the enemy that persecuted us. (19) And thou hast taken pity upon two only children. Make them, O Lord, bless thee more fully : and to offer up to thee a sacrifice of thy praise, and of their health, that all nations may know that thou alone art God in all the earth.

† J. (21 and 22) reads : And he spoke to his wife to make ready a feast and prepare all kinds of provisions that are necessary for such as go on a journey. (22) He caused also two fat kine and four wethers to be killed, and a banquet to be prepared for all his neighbours and all his friends.

‡ J. reads (5): And indeed thou seest how Raguel had adjured me, whose adjuring I cannot despise.

thee, for thou art the son of a good man, Godfearing and avoiding evil. **9** (10, 11) May thy house be as the house of Perez, who begat Hezron.* (12) And all the people answered: Amen! and they ate and drank and made merry.

X. **1** (1–3) But Tobi was heavy and wretched, and it grieved him at his heart, and he said: my son, my son, why dost thou tarry, why are thy steps so long in coming?† Such was his custom all the days. **2** (4) And Hanna wept and did not eat, for her sighs were many and her heart was faint. **3** And she said to her husband: thou are verily guilty of this great tribulation which thou hast brought upon us, **4**‡ for thou hast sent away our son, the joy of our heart, the nourisher of our old age, under whose shadow we would live among the nations. **5** (6) And Tobi answered her: fear not, my sister, for [I trust in the lovingkindness of my God, that he will bring him back] in peace, as the man who went with him is very trusty [and he is an angel from the Lord of hosts]. **6** (7)§ Go outside, my sister, and see, perhaps it might be the will of God, through his mercy, that thou bring me tidings and rejoice my fainting heart. Such was his custom all the time his son was abroad.‖ **7** (9) Tobiyah was thinking in his own heart, and he said to Reuel, his father-in-law: why dost thou make me tarry, and God has made my way prosperous, whilst the sleep has fled from my father and my mother, they do not rest nor are they still [until I return home in peace?]¶ **8** [But Reuel said to his son-in-law: be content, I pray thee, and tarry with me; fulfil these

* J. reads: (10) And may a blessing come upon thy wife and upon your parents; (11) and may you see your children and your children's children unto the third and fourth generation, and may your seed be blessed by the God of Israel who reigneth for ever.

† X. J. (1–3) reads: But as Tobias made longer stay upon occasion of the marriage, Tobias his father was solicitous, saying, Why thinkest thou doth my son tarry, or why is he detained there? (2) Is Gabelus dead, thinkest thou, and no man will pay him the money? (3) And he began to be exceeding sad both he and Anna his wife with him: and they began both to weep together, because their son did not return to them on the day appointed.

‡ J. (5) (here missing): We having all things together in thee alone, ought not to have let thee go from us.

§ J. (7) reads: But she could by no means be comforted, but daily running out looking round about, and went into all the ways by which there seemed any hope he might return, that she might if possible see him coming afar off.

‖ J. (8) (here missing) reads: But Raguel said to his son-in-law, stay here, and I will send a messenger to Tobias thy father, that thou art in health.

¶ J. (9): And Tobias said to him, I know that my father and mother now count the days, and their spirit is grievously afflicted within them."

two weeks, and I will send thee away with mirth and with song. 9 But Tobi answered: no, my lord, listen to me, and send me away, so that I go to my country, and my wife with me.] 10 (10) When Reuel saw that he could not prevail upon him, he sent him away, and his wife with him, with silver and gold, and precious things, and cattle, and great household, and with great mirth. 11 (11)* And Reuel blessed his daughter, and said: may the Lord God of Israel give unto thee seed of men, and prosper thy way! †

XI. 1 And they sent him away, and his wife [and all his relations and friends and acquaintances went with him one day's journey, and they gave him gifts, everyone a ring of gold, a Qesitah and a piece of silver; (1) and they went on their way to the city of Nineveh.] 2 (2) And when they came near the city, the angel of the Lord said to Tobiyah: thou knowest that it is a long time since we have separated ourselves from your father. 3 (3) Set thy steps on thy walk and go quickly to thy father, and I will lead on softly according to the pace of the flock. 4 (4) And Tobiyah said: the word is good which thou hast spoken. And he hastened and saddled his ass, and he arose and went.‡ 5 (7) And the angel charged Tobiyah: as soon as thou shalt come into the house, forthwith give thanks to God and bless him, and go to thy father and kiss him. 6 (8) And the gall of the fish which thou hast put up to keep, take with thee and anoint the eyes of thy father, and he will see, and his heart will rejoice. 7 Then Tobiyah went away from him and came into the town; (5)§ when he came near his mother perceived him (6)|| and she ran and told it to her husband.¶ 8 (10) And Tobi

* J. (11): "saying, the holy angel of the Lord be with you in your journey, and bring you through safe. and that you may find all things well about your parents, and my eyes may see your children before I die."

† J. adds (12–13): And the parents taking their daughter kissed her and let her go. (13) Admonishing her to honour her father and mother-in-law, to love her husband, to take care of the family, to govern the house, and to behave herself irreprehensibly.

‡ J. reads (4): And as their going pleased him, Raphael said to Tobias, Take with thee of the gall of the fish, for it will be necessary. So Tobias took some of that gall and departed.

§ J. (5): But Anna sat beside the way daily, on the top of a hill, from whence she might see afar off.

|| J. (6) And while she watched his coming from that place, she saw him afar off, and presently perceived it was her son coming.

¶ J. (9) omitted: Then the dog which had been with them in the way, ran before, and coming as if he had brought the news, showed his joy by his fawning and wagging his tail.

rejoiced exceedingly, and he arose from his bed and wanted to run to meet his son, and he dashed his foot against a stone [and he fell down, for his eyes were blind]. 9 And Tobiyah hastened (11) [and descended from the ass and lifted his father up from the ground] and kissed him, and they wept (12) and worshipped God ; they praised him and blessed him with a loud voice. 10 (13) And Tobiyah took the gall of the fish and annointed the eyes of his father with it (14, 15) and his eyes were opened ; and the white substance which covered the eyes fell off, and he rejoiced exceedingly.* 11 (16) When Hannah saw that her husband was seeing, she worshipped God. 12 (17) And she said : blessed be the Lord God of Israel, who has comforted us and has magnified his mercy.† 13 (18) And it came to pass after the completion of seven days that Sarah arrived with all the cattle and the young and the camels and beasts which her father Reuel had given her. 14 (19) And Tobiyah told his father all that had happened to him, and what the angel had done for him, and how God had prospered him.§

XII. 1 (1) And Tobi said to his son : in what manner shall we honour this man ? (2, 3) for all that thou hast, has come to thee through him. He has moreover killed the demon, and has done many wondrous things for thee ? 2 (4) And now, my son, call him, that he may take one half of the riches which thou hast brought. 3 (5) And he listened to his father, and called the angel. And he besought him and said : I pray thee, my Lord, man of God, behold the Lord has blessed me for thy sake : choose thee from all that I possess, and take one half thereof. (6) And he answered : I will not take anything ; 4 but do ye serve God with fear, and worship him and praise his holy name, for he renders to every man according to his work. 5 And blessed be now the Lord who has rendered thee thy reward, for thou hast acted towards the dead in piety and in truth. 6 And the strength of Israel will not lie or utter falsehood, for

---

* J. (14 and 15) : (14) And he stayed about half an hour ; and a white skin began to come out of his eyes, like the skin of an egg (15) and Tobias took hold of it and drew it from his eyes, and immediately he recovered his sight.

† J. (17) : And Tobias said, I bless thee, O Lord God of Israel, because thou hast chastised me, and thou hast saved me : and behold I see Tobias my son.

§ J. (20 and 21) omitted in our text. (20) And Achior and Nabath the kinsmen of Tobias came rejoicing for Tobias, and congratulating with him for all the good things that God had done for him. (21) And for seven days they feasted and rejoiced all with great joy.

he is truthful. **7** (9) And righteousness (alms) delivers from death.*
8 (13) And God has tried thee and has brought upon thee tribulations,
and has purified thee as silver and has heard thy prayer. **9** (15) And
he has sent me, the angel Raphael, one of the seven princes who
minister first in the presence of the King, the Lord of hosts.
10 (14) And he commanded me to heal thee and to save thee and to
conduct thy son and to bring him back ; for God had listened to thy
prayer and to thy reproach, and to the prayer and reproach of Sarah.
11 (16) And when they had heard his words, they were amazed one
at another, and they fell down upon their faces. **12** (17) And he said
to them, fear not,† (18) for I came by the word of God, and by his
command have I done all these things [and not by any will of mine],
(19) and behold, at the sight of your eyes I appeared to eat and
drink,‡ and yet did I neither eat bread nor drink water.§ **13** (21,
22) So they arose and blessed God, and the angel had disappeared,
and they did not know it (see it), for they feared that they would die,
as their eyes had seen an angel of the Lord of hosts.

XIII. **1** (1) And they arose and blessed God the Lord their God.
And Tobi said : blessed art thou, O Lord, and great are thy works,
and thou shalt reign for ever and ever. **2** (2) For [thine is the
kingdom], thou leadest down to Sheol and bringest up again, he
wounds and he heals, and there is none who could deliver out of
his hand. **3** (3)‖ O give thanks unto the Lord, for he is good : for his
mercy endureth for ever. **4** Who can utter the mighty acts of the
Lord, or show forth all his praise ? unto thee praise shall be given.
5 Bless the Lord, O my soul, O Lord my God, thou art very great ;
thou art clothed with honour and majesty. **6** Blessed be the
Lord God of Israel from everlasting even to everlasting. And all

---

* J. (6-13) corresponding to end of **3** and **4–7** differs greatly ; J. (7–8) and
(10–12) are missing here. (7) For it is good to hide the secret of a king : but honour-
able to reveal and confess the works of God. (8) Prayer is good with fasting and
alms, more than to lay up treasures of gold. (10) But they that commit sin and
iniquity, are enemies to their own soul. (11) I discover then the truth unto you
and I will not hide the secret from you. (12) When thou didst pray with tears,
and didst bury the dead, and didst leave thy dinner, and hide the dead by day
in thy house, and bury them by night, I offered thy prayer to the Lord.

† J. adds, Peace be to you.

‡ J. reads : but I use an invisible meat and drink, which cannot be seen by
men.

§ J. (20) omitted here : It is time therefore that I return to him that sent me :
but bless ye God, and publish all his wonderful works.

‖ **(3)** till end of chapter totally different from J.

the people say : Amen ! **7** And it came to pass that before they had finished their repast Tobiyah was told : lo, thy wife has come with the cattle and the flock. And they arose and went to meet them with timbrels and dances, and they brought them into the house with mirth and songs. **8** And they fulfilled the days of the feast, and they blessed God with a loud voice : Oh that men would praise the Lord for his loving kindness, and for all the good deeds and the wondrous things which God has wrought for us. **9** And Tobi said : blessed art thou, oh Lord God of Israel, because thou hast not denied us thy love and thy truth, thou who art the keeper of the covenant, and of the love for those who love thee and keep thy covenant. **10** And Tobi said to his son and to his wife Sarah, O give thanks unto the Lord, call upon his name ; make known his doing among the peoples, because he has dealt wondrously with us, and has changed our mourning into mirth, and our sorrow into dance and a day of feasting. And all the people answered : Amen ! and Tobi said to his son Tobiyah : blessed be our Lord, of whose gifts we have eaten, and through whose goodness we live. And all the people answered : blessed be our Lord, of whose gifts we have eaten, and through whose goodness we live. **12** And all the people arose and blessed Tobi and his wife, and Tobiyah his son, and his daughter-in-law, and they said to Tobiyah : may thy house be like unto the house of Perez. And they answered : Amen ! And they went, everyone of them, to their tents, joyful and glad of heart.

   XIV. **1** (1) And Tobi lived after he had recovered his sight forty-nine years, and the days of his life were one hundred and seventy years. **2** (2) And he died and was gathered unto his people in a good old age in the city of Nineveh.* **3** (4) And the rest of his works were in the love of God, in gladness of heart and abundance in everything, and in the fear of God and clinging to him. **4** (5) And it was before his death, and he spake to his son, saying : come near to me, my son, and do not stand aside, for I will counsel thee before God, ere I (die). . . . .

BE STRONG.

---

* J. (3) omitted here : For he was six and fifty years old when he lost the sight of his eyes, and sixty when he recovered it again.

C

TOBIT LEGEND II (H.G).

Thou shalt surely tithe all the increase of thy seed, that which cometh forth of the field year by year.   And thou shalt eat before the Lord thy God, in the place which he shall choose to cause his name to dwell there, the tithe of thy corn, of thy wine, and of thine oil, and the firstlings of thy herd and of thy flock ; that thou mayest learn to fear the Lord thy God always.   Our sages say : " Thou shalt surely tithe " (Asser te 'asser), which means : tithe in order that thou become rich, and tithe surely, in order that thou have no wants.   This is an indication to those that travel on the high seas to give the tenth to those that are engaged in the study of the law.   If thou tithest then it is thy corn, but if not, it is my corn, as it is said (Hosea ii, 11), " therefore will I take back my corn in its due time."   If thou art worthy, it is thy wine, but if not, it is mine.   Rabbi Levi said : (Prov. xxviii, 22) " He that hath an evil eye hasteth after riches, and knoweth not that want shall come upon him," this verse applies to the man who does not bring out his tithes in a proper manner.   For R. Levi said : It happened once (a history is told) of a man who brought out his tithes in a proper manner (etc.), therefore Moses warned the Israelites to tithe surely.

1. The history is told of a man whose name was Tobi, of the tribe of Napthali, who all his days walked in the right path, and performed many good deeds for his brethren who were with him in the captivity in Nineveh : and he was left an orphan by his father, and he was brought up by Deborah his father's mother, and she led him in the right path.   And when he became a man he took a wife of his own kindred and family, whose name was Hannah, and she bare him a son, and he called his name Tobiyah.   And when he was in the captivity, in the city of Nineveh, all his brethren and kindred polluted themselves, and did eat the bread of the sons of the Gentiles.   But he did not eat, for he feared God with all his heart.   And therefore God gave him grace and favour in the eyes of Shalmanesser, the king, and he appointed him master over all that he had, to the day of his death.   And at that time he committed to the hand of Gabael his kinsman ten talents of gold.   And after the death of the king Shalmanesser, his son Sennacherib reigned in his stead.   And in the days of Sennacherib Tobi did many

charitable deeds for the poor, and he fed the hungry and the orphans; and when he saw one of the Jews slain, cast out in the street, he buried him. Now when Sennacherib returned in haste from Judah, he went to Nineveh in fierce wrath against the ten tribes, and killed many of them, and their corpses were cast out in the streets, and none buried them. When Tobi saw that, his wrath was kindled, and he arose in the night and buried them; and thus he did many times. Once Sennacherib asked for the bodies of the slain, but found them not. And the men of Nineveh said to the king: Tobi buries them. And the king commanded that he be put to death. When Tobi heard it, he fled. And the king commanded that they should pillage his house, and he hid himself from him five and forty days, until Adramelech and Sharezer his sons killed Sennacherib with the sword, and Esarhaddon his son reigned in his stead. And the king appointed Aqiqar over all his affairs. And Aqiqar spake good words for Tobi, and he brought him back to Nineveh.

II. When the feast of Weeks came, his wife prepared a plentiful meal, and as he sat at the table, he said to his son Tobiyah: go, and bring to me some of our poor brethren, such as fear God, to eat with us. Then Tobiyah went and found a man slain, cast out in the street, and he told his father. What did his father do? he rose from the table and he went with him, and he took him from the street of the city, and brought him into a house until the going down of the sun, that he might be able to bury him. And he turned to his house and ate his bread in mourning. And he said: Woe that on us is fulfilled, "and I will turn your feasts and your songs into mourning." And he wept very sore. And when the sun went down he went and buried him. And he returned to his house, and he lay upon his bed, and his face was uncovered, and dust fell from the wall into his eyes. And in the morning he went to the physician to cure his eyes, but it did not avail him, until he became blind of both eyes, which lasted for four years. And Aqiqar his friend nourished him. After many days his wife did work for women, and they gave her a kid for her wages. And Tobi heard the kid bleating in the house, and he asked her: from whence hast thou this kid? hast thou stolen it perhaps? And his wife Hannah said: they have given it to me as the wages of the work of mine hands; I have not stolen it! But Tobi did not believe her, and they quarrelled concerning the kid. Hannah said to Tobi: Where are thy goodnesses and thy merits? hence thy worthlessness is manifest to all!

III. When Tobi heard this he was much grieved, and he wept and prayed to the Holy One, blessed be he, in the anguish of his soul, and he said: Lord of the universe! take my soul from me, for it is better for me to die than to live, so that I shall no more hear shame. And the same day, Sarah, the daughter of Reuel, who lived in Agbatanis, in the land of Media, heard a great reproach because she had been given to seven men as wife, and not one of them came in unto her according to the way of all the earth. And her maid said to her: it is thou who hast killed these men to whom thou hast been given in marriage, and not one of them has come in unto thee because thou hast hurt them. And it came to pass, when Sarah heard the words o her maid she wept very much, and went up into the upper chambei to pray there in the anguish of her soul. And she said: Lord of the universe! thou knowest that I am pure, and I have not polluted myself with man. I am the only daughter of my father, neither has he son to inherit his property, nor any kinsman; and behold, seven husbands are dead for my sake, and why should I live? But if it please not thee to kill me, have pity on me that I hear no more reproach! Our sages say that on that day the Holy One, blessed be he, accepted their prayers, and he commanded the angel Raphael to heal them both; to cure Tobi from the blindness of his eyes, and to give Sarah for wife to Tobiyah, the son of Tobi, and to take away from her Ashmedai, the king of the demons.

IV. At that time Tobi remembered the money which he had committed to the hand of Gabael. And he called his son Tobiyah, and said to him, My son, fear the Lord thy God all thy days, and give alms all thy days, and do not walk with a thief or an adulterer, and set aside thy tithes as is proper, and the Holy One, blessed be He, will give thee great riches. And now, my son, know that I have committed ten talents of silver to the hand of Gabael, and I know not the day of my death; go to him, and he will give thee the money.

V. And Tobiyah answered his father: All that thou hast commanded me I will do: but how can I take the money from the hand of Gabael, who knoweth me not, and I know not him? His father said to him: Take this ring, which he has given me, and I have given him my ring. And now, my son, seek thee a trusty man, who may go with thee, and I will give him his wages. So Tobiyah went immediately to seek for a man who might go with him, and he found the angel Raphael standing by. But he did not recognise him that he was an angel of the Lord. He asked him : From whence art thou ? He answered him, From the Children of Israel. He said to him : Knowest thou how to go to Media ? And he said : Yes. Tobiyah said to him : Tarry a little for my sake, and I will tell my father. Tobiyah went and told his father. He said to him : Call him. And he said to him : My son Tobiyah desireth to go to Media ; art thou willing to go with him ? He said to him : Yes ! And Tobi called his son immediately, and said to him : Prepare thyself, and go with this man, and may the Lord of heaven prosper your way and bring you back in peace.

VI. Both went then on their journey, and they came to the river Euphrates, and they passed the night there. And Tobiyah ran to the river to drink, and a fish came out and ate his bread, and he cried out. And Raphael said to Tobiyah : Lay hold of the fish, and do not let it go. Tobiyah went and laid hold of the fish and drew it out, and Raphael said to him : Open it in the middle and take its heart ; it is good to burn it before a man in whom the spirit of demons is, to make them flee from him ; and take also the gall, for it is good to anoint therewith the eyes in which there is blindness, and they shall be healed. So Tobiyah did as the angel commanded him, and they went to Media. And Raphael said to Tobiyah : My brother, thou comest to the house of Reuel, who is an old man, and has a daughter who is exceeding fair, whose name is Sarah, speak to him that he may give her to thee for a wife. Tobiyah said to him : I have heard that she has been given in marriage to seven men, and they died before they came in unto her. Raphael said : Fear not ! when thou shalt be with her in the marriage chamber, take the heart of the fish and burn thereof under her garment, and the demon will smell it, and will run away.

VII. Raphael said to Reuel : Give thy daughter to Tobiyah for a wife. And he said : I am willing. And Reuel took his daughter Sarah and gave her to Tobiyah for a wife. And Reuel said to his wife : Prepare a bedchamber. Tobiyah and his wife Sarah went into it ; and Tobiyah remembered the words of Raphael, and he took the heart of the fish and put it on a censer and burnt it under the clothes of Sarah. And Ashmedai received the smell, and he fled instantly ; and both prayed to the Holy One, who had healed her. On the morrow, Tobiyah said to Raphael : Go to

Gabael, that he may give thee ten talents of gold.   Raphael went immediately, and brought the money; and Raphael said to Tobiyah : Thou knowest that thou hast left thy father and thy mother in great pain; now let us go to prepare the house, and let thy wife come after us.   So they both of them went.   Raphael said to Tobiyah : When thou comest into the house of thy father, take the gall and put it in the eyes of thy father, and he will be cured.   He did so.   And Tobi said to his son : Tell me all that thou hast done.   And he told him.   And he said : Blessed be the Lord who hath sent his angel with my son, and hath prospered his way, and hath cured two poor people like ourselves.   In after days God blessed Tobiyah also, because he fulfilled the command of his father, and gave tithes of everything that he possessed.

Hence we learn how great is the power of alms and tithes, and how, because Tobi gave alms and separated his tithes as is meet, the Holy One, blessed be he, rewarded him !   And because the Patriarchs of the world knew the power of alms and tithes they were careful in observing them.   Therefore did Moses warn the Israelites, saying to them : Thou shalt surely tithe all the increase of thy seed.

HARRISON AND SONS, PRINTERS IN ORDINARY TO HER MAJESTY, ST. MARTIN'S LANE, LONDON.

ut, so that; so also X, 5. — 16: ביראת אלהיך v. III, 19. —
בקריאת הגבר cockcrowing. Postbiblical.

VII, 17: וישמחו בשמחה — שמחה.

VIII, 9: זכרה נא לנו לחסדיך (construed with ל, so also
v. 10, and similarly יאמינו הלבבות). — 15: לבלתי לנגוע — נגוע).
— 19: בכל הקטים cf. Deut. 6, 22.

XI, 3: ובאה את אביך — אל. — 6: ושמח בלבו — לבו.
9: וישתחו אל ה' — לה'.

XII, 2: כל מחצית — מחצית כל. — 10: חרפתך: the reproach
with which thou hast been reproached and so ibid. חרפתה.

XIII, 11: ברוך שאכלנו משלו.

———

אביך ואת אמך בצער גדול · ועתה נלך אנחנו לפנות הבית ותבא אשתך

אחרינו · וילכו שניהם · אמ' רפאל לטוביה כשתבא לבית אביך קח המרה

95 מן הדג וישם (ושם .l) בעיני אביך וירפא · ויעש כן ואמר טובי לבנו סימר (!)

לי כל מה שעשית ויספר לו · ואמר ברוך י"י ששלח מלאכו עם בני

והצלח דרכו ורפא שני עניים כמונו · לאחר ימים ברך אלהים לטוביה

על שקיים מצות אביו ויתן מעשר מכל אשר לו · הא למדנו כח הצדקות

והמעשרות כמה גדול על שעשה טובי צדקות והפריש מעשרותיו כראוי

100 מה שלם לו הבה ולפי שהיו יודעין אבות העולם כח הצדקה והמעשרות

היו זהירין בהן · לכך הזהיר משה עשר תעשר את כל תבואת זרעך:

Peculiar forms and constructions in the Hebrew Text A. of Tobit, some of which are postbiblical.

I, 6: וישפך לבו עליו (v. VIII, 4. cf. Lament. 2, 19. Ps. 62, 9). — 10: בא במדי (similar forms with ב: III, 11 ותעל בעלייה; IX, 2 לבא בשמחה = אל). — 17: הרגו סנחריב בניו.

II, 2 אחד נאמן. — cf. V, 2: כי אחד מבני ישראל ראה 7: הרבה יראתי (cf. Eccl. 1, 16. Ezra 10, 1. Nehem. 2, 2.). — 17: אגמול חסד עם המתים neologism. Biblical is: עשה חסד (v. Ruth I, 8). — 14: חיי העולם הבא (postbiblical). — 15: ותעש לרבים (= worked for many). — 17: פן גניבה (Conj. before a noun, not biblical).

III, 7: אוי לך ולמזלך (postbiblical idea of: luck). — 9: לא גומל לחייבים טובות (cf. v. 19. Nehem. 8, 10). — 15: נכונו אליה 21: והצדקה תעביר רוע הגוירה (later paraphrase of Prov. 10, 2. v. XII, 7).

IV, 1: מתחנן על נפשו instead of: וישאל את נפשו (I Kgs. 19, 4. Jonah 4, 8). — ויקרא לבנו לאמור = spake.

V, 2 s. II, 2. — 12: אל ירע לפני (biblical: בעיני cf. Gen. 21, 12). — 17: ושלח Perfect instead of Imperfect so also v. 19 ולא תאכל. cf. X, 2 ויהיו = והיו and ותן = ונתת VIII, 11 ונתן (= ויתן) = ולא אכלה. — 20: למהר לשוב cf. Exod. 12, 33.

VI, 1: לפי תומו = suddenly. Postbiblical. — 2: עוד יהיו ... = אשר יצאו. — 7: כל = יורשת בכל. — 15: לרפואה (cf. V, 24). —

קרוב והרי מתו בעדי שבעה אנשים ולמה יש לי חיים עוד • ואם לא 55
ייטב בעיניך להרוג אותי רחם עלי ולא אשמע חרפה עוד. אמרו חֹל"ל
כי ביום הזה קבל הָבֹה תפלתם • ושלח למלאך רפאל לרפאת את
שניהם את טובי מעורון עיניו ואת שרה ליתן לטוביה בן טובי לאשה
ולהסיר ממנה אשמדאי מלך השדים • IV. באותה שעה זכר טובי את
הכסף שהפקיד ביד נבאל • ויקרא לטוביה בנו ואמר לו• בני כל ימיך 60
את י"י אלהיך תירא ועשה צדקה כל ימיך ולא תלך עם איש גנב ונואף
והפריש מעשרותיך כראוי והַבֹה יתן לך עושר רב • ועתה בני דע כי
עשר ככר כסף הפקדתי ביד נבאל ולא ידעתי יום מותי • תלך אליו
והוא יתן לך הכסף • V. ויען טוביה אל אביו כל אשר צויתגי אעשה V.
אבל איך אוכל לקחת הכסף מיד נבאל הוא לא מכיר לי ואני לא מכיר 65
אותו • אמר לו אביו קח הטבעת הזאת שנתן לי • וטבעתי נתתי לו•
ועתה בני בקש איש נאמן שילך עמך ואתן לו שכרו• מיד יצא
טוביה לבקש איש נאמן שילך עמו ומצא את המלאך רפאל עומד ולא
הכירו כי מלאך י"י הוא• שאל לו מנין אתה• אמ' לו מבני ישראל• אמר
לו ידעת להלוך למדי• אמר לו הן• אמר לו טוביה אמתין (המתין 1.) לי ואניד 70
לאבי• הלך טוביה וינד לאביו• אמר לו קרא אותו• אמר לו טובי בני
רוצה להלוך למדי רוצה אתה להלוך עמו• אמ' לו הן• מיד קרא טובי
לבנו ואמר לו התקין עצמך ותלך עם האיש הזה ואלהי השמים יצליח
דרככם ושבתם בשלום • מיד הלכו שניהם בדרך ויבואו עד הנהר פרת
וילינו שם VI. וירץ טוביה אל הנהר לשתות ויצא דג ואכל לחמו VI.
וצעק • ואמר רפאל לטוביה לך ואחוו את הדג ולא תעזוב אותו• הלך 75
טוביה ותפש אל (את 1.) הדג ויוצא אותו ליבשה• אמר לו רפאל בצע אותו
באמצע וקח לבו והוא טוב להקטיר ממנו לפני כל איש שיש בו רוח
שדים שיברחו ממנו • וקח המרה והיא טובה למשוח ממנה העינים
שיש בהם עורון וירפאו • עשה כן טוביה כאשר צוה לו רפאל וילכו עד 80
מדי • ואמר רפאל לטוביה• אחי לבית רעואל תבא שהוא איש זקן ולו
בת אחת יפה עד מאד ושמה שרה ואמור לו שיתן אותך לו (אותה לי.1)לאשה•
אמר לו טוביה שמעתי שהיא נשאת לשבעה אנשים וימותו בטרם
שבואו אליה • אמר רפאל לא תירא כאשר תהיה בחדר עמה קח לב
הדג וקטר אותה תחת בנדיו (בנדיה 1.) והשד מריח ויברח • VII. אמר רפאל VII.
לרעואל תן בתך לטוביה לאשה אמר לו הגני• ויקח רעואל את שרה 85
בתו ויתן לה לטוביה לאשה • אמר רעואל לאשתו אתקיני אדרון בית
משכבא ויבואו שמה טוביה ושרה אשתו• מיד זכר טוביה את דברי
רפאל ויקח לב הדג וישם על המתחה ויקטר תחת בגדי שרה ואשמדאי
קבל הריח וברח• מיד התפללו שניהם להָבֹה שרפא אותה• למחר אמר 90
טוביה לרפאל לך לנבאל ויתן לך העשרה ככרי זהב • מיד הלך רפאל
והביא את הכסף ואמר רפאל לטוביה אחי אתה ידעת איך הנחת את

ירא מן הֹבֹה בכל לבו ועל זאת נתן לו אלהים חן וחסד בעיני

שלמנאצר המלך ויפקוד אותו על כל אשר לו עד יום מותו • ובעת

ההיא צוה טובי ביד גבאל קרובו עשר כברי זהב • ואחר שמת שלמנאצר

20 המלך מלך סנחריב בנו תחתיו • ובימי סנחריב היה עושה טובי חסדים

רבים לעניים • והיה נותן לחם לרעבים וליתומים וכשהיה רואה הרוג

נופל בארץ מן היהודים היה קובר אותו • וישב סנחריב בחפזון מיהודה

הלך לנינוה בחימה גדולה על עשר השבטים והרג מהם רבים והיה

גבלתם מושלכים בארץ ואין היה קובר אותם • וכשראה טובי כך חרה

25 אפו ויקם בלילה וקבר אותם וכזאת עשה פעמים רבות • פעם אחד שאל

סנחריב את פגרי ההרונים ולא מצא אתהם. ויאמרו אנשי נינוה למלך

טובי קבר אותם בלילה ויצו המלך לדרוג אותו • וכששמע טובי כן

ברח • ויצו המלך לשלול את ביתו ויתחבא מלפניו מ"ה ימים עד כי

אדרמלך ושנאצר(!) בניו הרגו אותו בחרב לסנחריב(!) וימלוך אסרחדון בנו

30 תחתיו • ויפקוד המלך לאקקר על כל אשר לו • ודבר אקיקר דברים

II. טובים על טובי וישיבהו לנינוה. II. וכשהגיע חג שבעות עשה אשתו

ארסטוון רב • וכשהיה יושב על השולחן אמר לטוביה בנו לך והבא

לי מאחינו העניים מיראי אלהים לאכול עמנו • וילך טוביה ומצא איש

אחד מת מושלך בדרך וינד לאביו • מה עשה אביו קם מן השולחן וילך

35 אתו ויקח אותו מן רחוב העיר ויביא אותו בבית אחד עד בא השמש

שיוכל לקברו וישב אל ביתו ויאכל לחמו באבל • ואמר אוי לנו שקים

בנו וההפכתי חגיכם וכל שיריכם לאבל • ויבך בכי נדול וכשבא השמש

הלך וקבר אותו וישב אל ביתו וישכב על ממתו ופניו גלויות ונפל

עפר מן הכותל על עיניו • ובבקר היה הולך לרופא לעשות רפואה בעיניו

40 ולא הועיל לו כלום עד שעור משני עיניו והיה עוד ד' שנים • ואקיקר

אוהבו היה מפרנגם אותו • לימים רבים חנה אשתו היה עושה מעשה

לנשים וגנתנו לה נדי אחד בשכרה וטובי שמע הנדי זועק בבית • ושאל

לה מנין לך הנדי הזה אולי גגבת אותו • אמרה חנה אשתו בשכר מעשה

ידי נתנו לי שלא גגבתיהו • ולא האמין טובי לה וירבו שניהם על

45 הנדי • אמרה חנה לטובי אן טובך וזכוותך וקלנך אתגלי לכולא •

III. III. כששמע טובי כך חרה אפו ויבך והתפלל להֹבה בצרת נפשו ואמר

רבֹשׁע קח את נפשי ממני כי טוב מותי מחיי ולא אשמע חרפה עוד •

וביום ההוא שרה בת רעואל שהיתה באנבתנים בארץ מדי שמעה

חרפה גדולה לפי שנשאת לשבעה אנשים לאשה • ואחד מהם לא בא

50 כדרך כל הארץ ואמרה לה שפחתה את היא שהרנת את האנשים

האלה שנשאת להם ואחד מהם לא בא אליך שאתה מלקה אותם •

ויהי כאשר שמעה שרה את דברי שפחתה ותבך בכי נדול ותעל אל העלייה

להתפלל שם בצרת נפשה • ואמ' רֹבֹשׁע אתה ידעת כי טהורה אני ולא

נטמאתי עם אדם • ואני יחידה לאבי ואין לו בן לרשת נחלתו ולא

9 והחסד לאוהביך ולשומרי בריתך: ויאמר טובי אל בנו ואל שרה אשתו׃
הודו ליהוה קראו בשמו הודיעו בעמים עלילותיו׃[1] כי הפליא לעשות
עמנו ויהפך אבלנו· לשמחה ואת ינוננו למחול וליום טוב׃[2] ויענו כל העם·
10 אמן· ויאמר טובי אל טוביה בנו ברוך אלהינו שאכלנו (משלו) ובטובו
חיינו· ויענו כל העם· ברוך הוא אלהינו שאכלנו משלו ובטובו חיינו׃[3]
11 ויקומו ויברכו את טובי ואת אשתו וטוביה בנו וכלתו· ויאמרו לטוביה·
יהי ביתך כבית פרץ· ויענו· אמן· וילכו איש לאוהליו שמחים וטובי לב·
XIV. ויחי טובי אחרי האירו עיניו תשע וארבעים שנה· ויהיו ימי חייו[1/2]
מאה ושבעים שנה: וימת ויאסף אל עמו בשיבה טובה בעיר גנוה·
ויתר מעשיו (אשר עשה?) באהבת יהוה בשמחת לבב· וברוב כל· וליראה
3 את יהוה ולדבקה בו׃[4] ויהי לפני מותו ויאמר אל בנו לאמר נשה אלי
בני אל תעמד כי איעצך לפני אלהים לפני........

חזק

B.

[ליום שני של שבועות·]

עשר תעשר את כל תבואת זרעך היוצא השדה שנה שנה ואכלת
לפני י״י אלהיך במקום אשר יבחר לשכן שמו שם מעשר דגנך ותירושך
ויצהרך ובכורות בקרך וצאנך למען תלמד ליראה את י״י אלהיך כל
הימים· אמרו חז״ל עשר תעשר· עשר בשביל שתתעשר· תעשר שלא
5 תתחסר· רמז למפרשי ים להוציא אחד מעשרה לעמלי תורה· אם תעשר
דגנך· ואם לאו דגני· שנא׳ לכן אשוב ולקחתי דגני בעתו· זכיתם
תירושך· ואם לאו תירושי· ר׳ לוי אמ׳ נבהל להון איש רע עין ולא
ידע כי חסר יבואנו· זה הפסוק אמ׳ כזה שאינו מוציא מעשרותיו
כראוי· דאמ׳ ר׳ לוי׃· מעשה באחד שהיה מוציא מעשרותיו כראוי·
I. לפני משה מזהור לישראל עשר תעשר· I. מעשה שהיה באיש אחד
10 ושמו טובי משבט נפתלי וכל ימיו הלך בדרך ישר והיה עושה עם אחיו
חסדים רבים לאשר עמו היו בגלות בנינוה· והוא נשאר יתום מאביו וינדל
(ותגדל 1.) אותו דבורה אם אביו והיא נהג אותו בדרך ישר· וכאשר היה
איש נשא אשה מזרעו וממשפחתו ושמה חנה ותלד לו בן ויקרא שמו
15 טוביה· וכאשר היה בגולה בעיר נינוה כל אחיו וקרוביו היו מטמאין
נפשם ואוכלים לחם מן בני האומות· והוא לא היה אוכל מפני שהיה

---

[1] Ps. 105, 1.   [2] cf. Jerem. 31, 13.   [3] Formula of Grace, Talmud Berachoth f. 49 b and 50 a.   [4] cf. Deut. 11, 22.

13 ישראל אשר נחם אותגו ויגדל לנו חסדו׃ ויהי אחר מלאת שבעת
הימים׃ ותבא שרה וכל המקנה והטף והגמלים והבהמה אשר נתן לה
14 רעואל אביה׃ ויספר טוביה לאביו את כל הקורות אותו ואת כל
XII. אשר עשה לו המלאך ואשר הצליחו האלהים׃ XII. ויאמר טובי אל

1 בגו׃ במה נכבד את האיש? כי כל הבא אליך בגללו׃ ויהרג את הרשע
2 והרבה נפלאותיו עמך׃ ועתה בני קרא אותו׃ ולקח כל מחצית רכושך
3 אשר הבאת׃ וישמע אל אביו ויקרא אל המלאך ויחל את פניו ויאמר
אחלי נא לפני אדני¹ איש האלהים׃ הנה ברכני יהוה בגללך² עתה בחר
4 לך מכל הנמצא לי קח מחצית הכל׃ ויאמר׃ לא אקח דבר׃ אך עבדו
את יהוה ביראה והשתחוו לו וברכו את שם קדשו׃ כי הוא ישלם לאיש
5 כפעלו׃ והנה ברוך יהוה אשר נתן לך שכרך אשר פעלת עם המתים
6 חסד ואמת³׃ ונצח ישראל לא ישקר׃ ולא ידבר כזב כי אמת הוא׃
7 8 וצדקה תציל ממות⁵׃ והאלהים נסה אותך ויבא עליך הצרות האלה
9 ויצרף אותך ככסף וישמע את תפילתך׃ וישלחני אני רפאל המלאך
אחד מן שבעה השרים המשרתים ראשונה את פני המלך⁶ יהוה צבאות׃
10 ויצו עלי לרפאות אותך ולהצילך ולהוליך את בנך וחרפתה׃ ויהי כשמעם את
11 את תפילתך ותרפתך עם תפלת שרה וחרפתה׃ ויהי כשמעם את
12 דבריו ויתמהו איש אל רעהו⁷ ויפלו על פניהם׃ ויאמר להם אל תיראו׃
כי בדבר יהוה באתי׃ ובמצותו עשיתי את כל הדברים האלה׃ כי לא
מלבי׃ והנה למראה עיניכם נראתי אוכל ושותה אבל לחם לא אכלתי
13 ומים לא שתיתי׃ ויקומו ויברכו את יהוה ויפרד המלאך והם לא
XIII. ידעו׃ כי יראו פן ימותו׃ כי מלאך יהוה צבאות ראו עיניהם׃ XIII. ויקומו

1 ויברכו את יהוה אלהיהם׃ ויאמר טובי׃ גדול אתה יהוה ונדולים מעשך⁸
2 ותמלוך עלינו לעולם ועד⁹׃ כי לך המלוכה מוריד שאול ויעל¹⁰׃ מוחץ
3 וידיו תרפינה׃ ואין מידו מציל¹¹׃ הודו ליהוה כי טוב כי לעולם חסדו¹²׃
4 מי ימלל גבורות יהוה ישמיע כל תהילתו כי לו דומיה תהילתהנ³ ברכו
5 נפשי את יהוה יהוה אלהי גדלת מאד הוד הדר לבשת¹⁴׃ ברוך יהוה
6 אלהי ישראל מהעולם ועד העולם׃ ואמר כל העם׃ אמן¹⁵׃ ויהי טרם כלו
לאכול ויונד למוביה הנה אשתך באה עם המקנה והצאן ויקומו וילכו
7 לקראתם בתופים ובמחולות׃ ויביאם הביתה בשמחה ובשירים¹⁶׃ וימלאו
ימי המשתה ויברכו את יהוה קול גדול׃ יודו ליהוה חסדו¹⁷ על כל
8 המובות והנפלאות אשר פעל לנו יהוה׃ ויאמר טובי׃ ברוך אתה יהוה
אלהי ישראל אשר לא מנעת חסדך ואמיתך מעמנו שומר הברית

---

1 II Kings 5, 3.   2 Gen. 30, 27.   3 cf. Ruth 1, 8.   4 I Sam. 15, 29.
5 Prov. 10, 2.   6 Esther 1, 13, 14.   7 Gen. 43, 33 cf. Is. 13, 8.
8 cf. Ps. 111, 2.   9 cf. Exod. 15, 18.   10 I Sam. 2, 6.
11 Deut. 32, 29.   12 Ps. 106, 1—2.   13 Ps. 65, 2.   14 Ps. 104, 1.
15 I Chr. 16, 36.   16 Gen. 31, 27.   17 Ps. 107, 8.

בני בני מדוע בושש אתה לבא ומדוע אחרו פעמיך¹ כה משפטו כל
הימים: ותבך חנה ולא תאכל כי רבות היו אנחתה ולכה דויֿ²: ותאמר 2 3
אל אישהֿ· אבל אשם אתה כי הבאת עלינו הצרה הגדולה הזאתֿ³:
תשלח את בנינו לבבינו המכלכל את שיבתינו אשר בצלוֿ⁴ 4
נחיה בגוים⁴: ויען לה טוביֿ· אל תיראי אחותיֿ· כי בחסדי אלהי בטחתי 5
אשר ישיבהו בשלוםֿ· כי האיש ההולך עמו נאמן מאדֿ· ומלאך יהוה
צבאות הואֿ: לכי נא החוצה אחותי וראיֿ· אולי יאבה יהוה בכל 6
צדקותיוֿ· ובשרתני ושמחת את לבבי הדוהֿ· כה משפטו כל ימי היות בנו
החוצה: וגם טוביה היה מחשב בלבו ואומר אל רעואל התגנוֿ· למה 7
תאחר אותי ויהוה הצליח דרכיֿ⁵· והנה אבי ואמי גדדה שנתם ולא ינוחו
ולא ישקוטו עד יום שובי בשלום: ויאמר לו רעואל להתגנוֿ· הואל נא 8
ושב אתי ומלא שבעים אלה ואשלחך בשמחה ובשרים⁶ֿ: ויען לו 9
טובי(ה)ֿ· לא אדני שמעניֿ· שלחני ואלכה (אל) ארצי ואשתי עמי:
זירא רעואל כי לא יכול לו וישלחהו זאת אשתו שלח עמו בכסף 10
וזוהב ובמגדנות⁷ ומקנה ועבודה רבה⁸ בשמחה גדולהֿ· ויברך 11
רעואל את בתו ויאמרֿ· יהוה אלהי ישראל יתן לך זרע אנשים ויהוה
יצליח דרכיך: XI. וישלחו אותו ואשתוֿ· וכל קרוביו ואהביו זמיזדעיו
הלכו עמו דרך יום אחדֿ· ויתנו לו מנתֿ· איש נזם זהב וקשטה , 1
ואגורה⁹ֿ· וישובו נגוה העירה: ויהי כאשר קרבו העירֿ· ויאמר מלאך 2
[אחד]⁹ᵃ יהוה אל טוביהֿ· הנה ידעת כי ארכו לנו הימים¹⁰ אשר
התפרדנו מאביך: זעתה שם לדרך פעמיך¹¹ זמהר ובאה את אביך¹ 3
זאני אתנהלה לאט לרגל אשתך ולרגל המקנה¹² ֿ: ויאמר לו טוביה 4
טוב הדבר אשר דברתֿ· וימהר טוביה ויחבש את חמורו ויקם וילך:
ויצו המלאך את טוביה בבואך הבית שם ליהוה תודה וברכהוֿ· 5
ובא לפני אביך ונשקתוֿ· זאת מרת הדג אשר הנתתה למשמרת קח 6
לך ומשח עיני אביךֿ· וראך ושמח בלבוֿ· וילך מאתו טוביה ויבא 7
העירה· זיהי בבאו ותראהו אמו ותרץ ותבשר את אישה: וישמח טובי 8
מאד ויקם מעל¹³ מטתוֿ· ויבקש לרוץ לקראת בנוֿ· ויגף באבן רגליו זיפל
ארצה· כי כהו עיניו· וימהר טוביה וירד מעל החמורֿ· ויקם את אביו 9
מעל הארץ וישקהוֿ· ויבכו וישתחו אל יהוה ויהללוהו ויברכוהו בקול
גדול: ויקח טוביה את מרת הדג וימשח בה את עיני אביו· ותפקחנה 10
עיני אביו ויפל הלובן אשר בסה [אשר כסה] את עיניו· וישמח מאד:
ותרא חנה כי ראה אישה ותשתחו (!) ליהוה: ותאמרֿ· ברוך יהוה אלהי 11 12

---

¹ cf. Judg. 5, 28.   ² Lam. 1, 22.   ³ cf. Gen. 42, 21.
⁴ Lam. 4, 20.   ⁵ Gen. 24, 56.   ⁶ Gen. 31, 27.   ⁷ 2 Chr. 21, 3.
⁸ cf. Job. 1, 3.   ⁹ Job 42, 11.   ⁹ᵃ So and sign of del. in MS.
¹⁰ Gen. 26, 8.   ¹¹ Ps. 85, 14.   ¹² Gen. 33, 14.
¹³ מ added afterwards over the word.   ¹⁴ Ps. 91, 12.

VIII

תפילתי לרצון לפניך· ואהיה דאויה לאיש חלו ומברכותיך תשלח לנו:

23 וינעה יהוה בשמן אשר לא ינע באדני זלא יעמד על ימונו לשטנו[1]:

24 על כן גדול יהוה אלהינו על כל ניסיך ונפלאותיך כי רבות המה· כי השמים ושמי השמים לא יכלכלוך[2] אף כי בני האדם לחקור אות

25 מהם: ומי ימלל את גבורותיך וישמיע כל תהילותיך[3]? ואתה הוא

26 המתנשא לכל לראש ומרומם על כל ברכה: ויהי בחצי הלילה בקריאת הגבר· ויקרא רעואל לאנשיו· קומו מהרו לחצוב קבר לטוביה· כי

27 ידעתי כי קרהו אסון כאשר לשבעת האנשים אשר התחתנו בי: זיהי ככלותו לחצוב הקבר· וישב רעואל אל ביתו ויאמר לאשתו· שלחי לי את

28 האמה וראתה והתבוננה אם הבחור חי או מת: ותלך האמה· והנה שנהם חיים שוכבים וישנים במטתם· ותשב ותבשרם בשורה טובה

29 וישמח לבבם: ויברכו את יהוה ויאמרו· ברוך יהוה אלהי ישראל אשר הטיב עמנו ומפליא לעשות[5]· ויגער בשטן אשר לא יכול להרע לנו ולבנינו· עד עולם וידעו כל הגוים אשר שמך נקרא עלינו[6]· ויצו רעואל

30 וימלאו את הקבר פה לפה: ויצו ויכינו טבח ויקרא אל כל שכניו[?]·

31 ויאכלו וישתו ויכרו כירה גדולה[7]: ויבקש רעואל פני טוביה לשבת

32 אתו עד שבועים: ויתן לו מחצית רכושו הונו ואוצרותיו וצאאנו[8] ואלפיו ושורו ועבודתו ובכל (וּמכל l.) אשר ימצא לו יתן לו (מחצית)

IX.

1 בחייו· ואחרי מותו יקח הכל: IX. ויאמר טוביה אל המלאך בי אדני אל יחר אפך בי· אך הפעם הואלתי דברי[9] והשבת חסדך

2 האחרון מן הראשון[10]: והלכת לי אל נבאל (!) אל המדינה (....) והאותות האלה קח בידך וקבל מאתו הכסף· ובקש ממנו לבא בשמחה ולשמוח עמנו· כי לא אוכל להפרד מזה עד מלאת שבועיים

3 תמימות ימי המשתה: ואתה ידעת כי לא ישקוט אבי ולא ינוח עד

4 שובי בשלום: וישמע לו המלאך· ויקח ארבעה מעבדי רעואל ושני גמלים אתו· ויבא דאגי ויתן אל נביאל האות· ויקח את הכסף מידו:

5 וינד לו את כל אשר לטוביה בן טובי ואשר בקש ממנו לבא לשמוח

6 עם הקרואים ביום חתונתו וביום שמחת לבו[11]: ויקם נבאל (!) ויחבש

7 את גמלו וילך אתו: ויהי בבא ביתה רעואל וימצאהו וטוביה עמו

8 יושבים על חלחם ויפל על צואריו וישקהו ויבך: ויברכהו ויאמר יברכך יהוה וישמרך[12] כי בן איש טוב וישר אתה· ירא אלהים וסר מרע[13]:

9 יהי ביתך כבית פרץ אשר הוליד את חצרון[14]· ויענו כל העם· אמן·

X.

1 ויאכלו וישתו וישמחו: X. והנה טובי סר וזעף ויתעצב אל לבו ויאמר·

---

1 Zech. 3, 1. 2 I Kings 8, 27. 3 Ps. 106, 2. 4 I Chr. 29, 11.
5 Judg. 13, 19. 6 Jerem. 14, 9. 7 II Kings 6, 23.
8 So Ms. on א a stroke i. e. deletur. 9 Gen. 18, 30. 10 Ruth 3, 10.
11 Song 3, 11. 12 Numb 6, 24. 13 Job 1, 1. 14 cf. Ruth 4, 12.

8 אלוה על כל· בורא הכל· גדול על כל· דורש הכל· הוא כל יכול·
ומרום על כל· זמר יתנו לו כל· חק ומצוה לכל· טוב לכל· ישר וצדיק
לכל· כל יכול· מורה לכל· נותנין לו שבח הכל· סומך הכל· עונה לכל·
פודה שבויי כל· צדיק וחסיד לכל· קרוב יהוה לכל· רחום יהוה
9 ורחמיו על כל· שירה יתנו לו כל· תומך שמו הכל¹: אלהי האלהים
ואדני האדנים [רחום] רחום נקרא שמך מעולם. זכרה נא לנו לחסדיך
10 ורחמיך כי מעולם המה²: וזכרה נא לי לחסדי טובי אבי אשר התהלך
לפניך בחסד ואמת והצילני ונער בשטן בלבתי לבלתי לנגוע ולהרע לנו:
11 ונתת לי מן האשה הזאת זרע אנשים³· והיו צאצאינו יודעי שמך ולומדי
תורתך⁴· ונודע בעמים כי אתה אלהים ואין עוד: ואתה השמים תשמע
12 תפילתי כאשר שמעת את תפילת אבותינו הקדושים את תפילת אברהם
באור כשדים· ותפילת יצחק בהר המוריה· ותפילת יעקב בביתאל·
ותפילת כל הישרים ושימם דמעתי בנאדך⁵ יהיו לרצון אמרי פי והגיון
13 לבי לפניך יהוה צורי וגואלי⁶: ותתפלל שרה ותאמר· יהוה יהוה אל
רחום וחנון ארך אפים ורב חסד ואמת נוצר חסד לאלפים לשמרי
14 עדותיו ומצותיו⁷: יהוה אחד לבדך ואין שני עמך· מי כמוך· ומי ידמה לך·
15 ומי ישוה לך· אין זולתך ואין בלתך· ואין ערוך אליך⁸: אתה בראת
הכל· ואין לפניך שכחה· לכן יאמינו הלבבות כי אתה אחד ונפלא בכל
דרכיך ונעלם מעין כל· ועין לא תשורך· ואתה היית עד לא היות
העולם· ואתרי אובדו תהיה· ושנותיך לא יתמו⁹· הן כל צבא השמים
16 בדברך נעשו וידך לא הויה בם לבראותם אך קראת ויעמדו יחדו ובידך·
17 הכח והגבורה להחליפם ולהאבידם ולהשיבם לקדמתם: ובידך החיים
והטוב ובראת העולם הזה לבחון בו בני האדם בחקים ובמשפטים אשר
18 צויתם: והעולם הבא בראת לחסדיך לאוהביך ולשומרי בריתך· ומאתמול
19 ערכת תפתה¹⁰ לזרים הבוגדים בך: ואתה הוא האלהים אשר בחרת
בזרע ישורון מכל העמים אשר על פני האדמה· ותעש להם אותות
20 ומופתים בכל הקמים עליהם¹¹: ועתה יהוה· מלך מלא רחמים· האזינה
תפילתי ואל דמעתי אל תחרש· כאשר שמעת אל תפילת אמינו שרה
בהתפללה על אודות [הגר] הנר שפתחה· ותפילת רבקה בהתרוצץ
21 הבנים בקרבה: וכתפילת רחל(!) אם הבנים עקרת הבית בעת כעסתה
אחותה ותפתח את רחמה ותלד בנים עומדים בחצרותיך לשרתך(!):
22 וכתפלת מרים הנביאה· וכתפלת אשת אלקנה כעסתה צרתה גם כעם
לבעבור הרעימה¹²· ותעמיד ממנה בן נביא עומד ומשרת לפניך· כן תעלה

---

¹ Poem with an alphabetical Acrostic.   ² Ps. 25, 6.   ³ I. Sam. 1, 11.
⁴ cf. Daily Prayers, taken from Talmud Tr. Berachoth f. 11 b.
⁵ Ps. 56, 9.   ⁶ Ps. 19, 15.   ⁷ Exod. 34, 6.
⁸ Liturgy Sabbath morning prayer (Nishmath).   ⁹ Ps. 102, 28.
¹⁰ Jes. 30, 33.   ¹¹ Deut. 6, 22.   ¹² I. Sam. 1, 6.

לילה ולילה תבעיר את הלב באש והעלית את עשנו על המטה אשר
15 תשכבו בה ונם הרשף: והיה בלילה הראשון• והזכרת שמות האבות
הקדושים• ובלילה השני התפלל אל אלהיך אשר יצאו מכם אנשים
16 טובים: והיה בלילה השלישי בקריאת הגבר ועשה רצונך ביראת אלהיך
VII. ויצליחך: [חצץ] VII. ויבאו אל בית רעואל וישמח מאד• וישק אל טוביה
1 ויאמר אל עדנה אשתו• הנה תארו כתואר איש הטוב טובי: ותאמר
2 אשתו• מי אתם• ומאין אתם? ויאמר מארץ נפתלי מן השביה אשר
3 בגינוה: ויאמר להם רעואל• הידעתם את טובי אחי? ויאמר המלאך
4 ידענו• וזה הבחור בנו• ושמו טוביה: וילך רעואל ויפל על פניו ארצה
5 וישקהו ויבך על צואריו• ויאמר• ברוך אתה בני ליהוה[2] כי בן איש טוב
אתה• ותבאנה עדנה אשתו (ובתו) ויבכו עליו• ויכינו לו מטבח[3]• וישחטו
6 שעיר עזים וישבו על הלחם[4]: וטוביה אמר אל רעואל• דודי•
שאלה גדולה אנכי שואל מעמך• כי אדני אל נא אל תשוב (תשיבי 1.):
7 ועתה הואל נא ותנה לי בתך לאשה• כי טוב תתה לי לאשה מתתה
8 לאיש אחר[5] כי עצמך ובשרך אני[6]• ויהל רעואל כי ירא פן ימות גם
הוא כשבעה אנשים המומתים על ידה• וישמר (וישם 1.) לפיו מחסום[7]:
9 ויאמר המלאך• אל תירא כי בא גד[8] ובשם יהוה תנה לו כי לא
נכונה לה וזה נכון• ויען רעואל לו יהי כדברך אדני• ויתן יהוה אלהי
10 ישראל את ביתם כבית פרץ[9]• וימלא את משאלות לכם ותאותם
לטובה• ואלהי אברהם יצחק ויעקב אבתינו יהיה עמהם ויצוה ברכתו
11 על שגיבם (שניהם 1.)[10]: ויאספו זקני העיר שם ויכתבו את הדברים•
ויברכו את האלהים והחתן והכלה• ויאכלו וישמחו בשמחה גדולה:
VIII. ויהי אחרי כן ויבאו שניהם החדרה הפנימית: ויזכר טוביה את
1 2 דברי המלאך• ויקח את הכבד• ויתן על נחלי אש• ויעל עשנו• ויקח המלאך
3 את הרשף ויאסרהו• וישלחהו המדברה אשר על פני מצרים: ויאמר
טוביה אל שרה• קומי והתפללי אל יהוה אלהינו הלילה גם בלילה
השני• והיה בלילה השלישי נתחברה יחדו כי בני קדושים אנחנו ולא
4 נלך בחקות הגוים אשר סביבותינו: ויקומו שניהם ויתפללו באימה
5 לפני יהוה• וישפכו את לבם להפיל תחנתם לפניו: ויאמר טוביה• ברוך
אתה יהוה אלהינו מלך העולם אשר ברא ששון ושמחה חתן וכלה:
6 ברוך אתה יהוה אלהינו מלך העולם אשר בראת את האדם בצלמך
7 ובתבניתך[11]• ונתת לו מכח גבורתך לדעת דעתך ולעבדך• ונתת לו עזר
כנגדו• וצוית להם לפרות ולרבות ולהרבות צאצאיהם בקרב הארץ:

---

1 Gen. 46, 29.   2 cf. Judg. 17, 2.   3 cf. Is. 14, 21.
4 cf. Gen. 37, 25.   5 I. Kings 2, 16.   6 cf. Gen. 29, 14. 19.
7 Ps. 39, 2.   8 Gen. 30, 11.   9 cf. Ruth 4, 12.   10 cf. Deut. 28, 8.
11 cf. Wedding Ritual; v. Talmud Ketuboth fol. 8a.

המלאך הגני· אלך עמו: ויאמר לו טובי· הגידה לי מה שמך ומאיזה 15
משפחה ושבט אתה?: ויען המלאך ויאמר· שמי עזריה בן חנניה הגדול· 16
ממשפחה נדולה אני· ויאמר טובי· אל יחר בעיניך והגדת לי מאיזו משפחה 17
אתה?: ויאמר משבט.... ויאמר לו טובי· האלהים יהיה עמכם ושלח 18
מלאכו לפניכם· ויכינו צדה לדרך וילכו שניהם יחדו: ותלך תנה אמו 18
מחוץ לעיר הלוך ובכה: ותאמר אליהם· האלהים יהיה עמכם ונתן 19
לכם חסד ורחמים לפני יושבי הארץ· ועתה הכן פעמיך למהר לשוב 20
אלינו לראות פנינו טרם מותינו (והורדנו) בינון שאולה: ויהי בשובה לביתה 21
ותאמר אל טובי מה זאת עשית כי שלחת את בנך את יחידך אשר
אהבת מעליך?: והיה אם יקראנו אסון והורדנו את שיבתינו בינון 22
שאולה[1]: כי בעוד בנינו אתנו היה לנו למשיב נפשינו ולכלכל את 23
שיבתינו[2]: ויען לה· אל תיראי אחותי· כי שלח יהוה מלאכו עמו והצליח 24
את דרכו והוא ישיבהו עוד·: VI. וילך טוביה עד הנהר חדקל וישב VI.
שם· וירד לרחוץ את רגליו· והנה דג נדול יוצא לקראתו לפי תומו 1
לבולעו· וירא ויקרא בקול נדול ויאמר· אדני הצילני מן הדג הגדול הזה:
ויאמר לו המלאך· קרעהו והוצאת לך לבו ומרירתו וכבדתו ושם לך 2
למשמרת· כי עוד יהיו לך לרפואה: ויקח את הדג ויבתר אותו בתוכו[3]· 3
ויאכלו את הבתר האחד· והשיני הצמיידו לדרך עד באם אל דאני אשר
במדינת מדי: וישאל הנער את איש האלהים· מה משפט הלב והכבד 4
והמרה אשר הנחנו למשמרת?: ויען לו· הלב קח לך· להוציא שדים מאיש 5
או מאשה כי תשרפנו באש· וישאלהו הנער· אנא נלין הלילה?: ויאמר 6
לו· בדאני העיר: והנה בעיר איש טוב ושמו רעואל ממשפחת אביך· 7
ואין לו בן או בת[5] רק בת אחת והיא יורשת בכל אשר לאביה· ובבאך 8
שם תשאלנה ממנו· כי לא ימנענה ממך: ויען טוביה ויאמר שמעני 9
וישמע לך האלהים: והנה לשמע אזן שמעתיה ותרגז בטני[6]· כי שמעתי 10
רבים מוציאי דבה· כי נתנה לשבעה אנשים ויהי בלילה הראשון לשכבם
יחד· ויבא ויבא אשמדאי מלך השדים בחצות הלילה ויהרגם: ועל כן וחלתי 11
ואירא[7] פן ישים נפשי כאחד מהם· והנה אני כמוה רך ויחיד לאבי ולאמי·
והיה אם יפגע בי (אסון) והורדתי את שיבתם בדם שאולה· ויאמר לו המלאך· 12
אל תערץ ואל תחת ואל ירך לבבך כי אודיעך במה תוציאהו מעליך: 13
ואתה דע לך· כי כל האנשים הממתים לא היו ראוים לה וליצא מהם
זרע אנשים על כן המיתם הרשף· ואתה עשה לך כאשר אצוך· והיו 14
יחד בחדר אחד שלשת ימים לילה ויום ואליה לא תקרב:: והיה מדי 15

---

1 cf. Gen. 42, 38.   2 Ruth 4, 15.   3 Gen. 15, 10.

4 The reading of these two words is uncertain; In the MS. it looks
like מלך חם which has no meaning.

5 cf. Judg. 11, 34.   6 Habk. 3, 17.   7 Job 32, 6.

טובי כי יחד התפללו• ותעל שועתם לפני האלהים וישלח מלאכ

IV. רפאל לרפאותם ולהצילם מצרתם: IV. והנה טובי מתחנן על נפשו

1 למות• ויקרא לבנו טוביה לאמר: שמע בני מוסר אביך ותורת אמך

2 לא תטש• והיה מוסרם ענוד על לבבך[2]: ובקהת אלהים את נפש

3 ונשאתני וקברתני בקבורת אבותי• ואת אמך כבד כל ימי חייך:

4 זכרת הצרות אשר עברו עלינו ועליה מדי יום יום• ובמלאת ימיה•

5 וקברת אותה בכבוד אצלי: וכל ימי חייך זכור בוראך[3] והשמר מחטוא

6 ומצות האלהים תשמר ותורתו: ופתוח תפתח לעני ידך• וכי תראה ערום

7 וכסיתו: הלא פרוש לרעב לחמך• ועיניך אל תעלים• מהם ויברכך האלהים

בכל מעשה ידיך ויפתח לך את אוצרו הטוב[5]• כי לא יועיל הון ביום

8 עברה וצדקה תציל ממות[6]• ואת האלהים ירא בכל נפשך ובכל מאדך•

9 ואל תתחבר לעושה עולה• ואל תשב במושב לצים: והשב לאיש פעלו

שכרו ביומו.תן• ואל ילין עמך שכר שכיר: ואהבת לרעך במך[7]• ועצת

10 צדיקים תדרוש: ועתה בני• לך לך ובקש ככרי הכסף אשר לי ביד

גביאל בעיר דאנו• והא לך האות אשר נתתי לו זכרון לכסף• ואל תירא

11 כי עמך האלהים בכל אשר תלך אם תשמר מצותיו: ואל יבהלוך הצרות

הגדולות אשר עברו עלינו• כי בטחתי [בירֹאת] ביראת האלהים כי עוד

V. תהיה לנו ישועה גדולה ורוח• על כן בני אל תירא: V. ויען טוביה

1 אל אבין ויאמר כל אשר תאמר• אלי אעשה• אך הוריני והדריכני בדרך

2 זו אלך: כי אני יחיד ואיככה אלכה לבדי להביא את הכסף: ויאמר לו

לך ובקש לי אחד נאמן בחוץ ואתן לו שכרו בעודני חי• והוא ילך עמך

3 לבקש הכסף: ויצא טוביה ביום ההוא וילך ויבקש בשוקי העיר איש

4 נאמן: ויצא לקראתו רפאל המלאך אשר שלחו האלהים להיות לו לעזר•

5 ולא ידע הנער כי מלאך האלהים הוא: וישאל לו הנער לשלום ויאמר

6 לו מי אתה אדני• ויען לו• מבני יהודה אני• ויאמר לו טוביה• הידעת דרך

7 ארץ נפתלי(!) ויאמר לו• ידעתי כל נבולי הארץ והמדינות: ומכיר אני את

גביאל איש משבטי והוא יושב בדאני העיר אשר במדי בעיר גנוה(!) בהר

8 אבתנים (אֲנְבְתָנִם 1.): ויאמר לו טוביה• אל יחר בעיניך אדני אלכה לאבי

9 ואשובה: וילך טוביה וינד לאביו• וישלח טובי אחרי האיש ויבא לפני

10 טובי וישאל לו לשלום: ויאמר לו המלאך• ששון ושמחה ישינוך[8]• ויאמר

11 לו• איזה שמחה תבא לי ואנכי יושב במחשכים כמתי עולם ואור השמש

12 אינני רואה: ויאמר לו• אל ירע לפני אדני כי קרובה ישועתך לבא

13 וראית ושמח לבך: ואמר לו טובי• הלא קראתי לך ללכת עם בני (אל)

14 גביאל היושב בדאני במדינת מדי• ובשובך אתן לך שכרך: ויאמר לו

---

1 Prov. I, 8. 2 Prov. 6, 21, 22. 3 cf. Eccles. 12, 1. 4 Jes. 58, 7. 8.
5 cf. Deut. 28, 12. 6 Prov. II, 4. 7 Levit. 19, 18.
8 Jes. 51, 11.

אתה וישר משפטיך ואורחותיך חסד ורחמים ואמת ומשפט׳ : ועתה יהוה 2

זכריני לטובה. ופקדיני בישועתיך² ואל תזכור לי עונות אבותי ומהר עניני 3

וחטאות אבותינו אל תזכור לי³ : כי על לא שמרנו מצותיך ותורתך היינו 4

למשל ולשנינה בכל הגוים אשר הבאתנו שמה⁴ : ועתה יהוה גדולים 5

מעשיך. והישר בעיניך עשה. והצור תמים עשה לי כחסדך חסד ואמת 6

ולקחת את נפשי כי מוב מותי מחיי : בעת ההיא ותהי שרה בת רעואל 7

אחי טובי מתפללת. ליהוה במדי : כי שמעה נאצות ובוזות ותקל בעיני 8

שפחה אחת לבית אביה : וכעסתה גם כעס⁵ מדי יום יום לאמר. אוי לך 9

ולמזלך כי שבעה אנשים נתנו לך וימותו כל אחד ואחד בלילה הראשונה 10

אשר באו אליך בכשפייך : ואיך נשאת עין ותרימי ראש לדבר אלי 11

קטנה או נדולה ואנכי מובה ממך : והנה שקר בפיה כי לא היתה ידה 12

במעל⁶. אך אשמדאי מלך השדים היה הורגם בלילה הראשונה על אשר 13

(לא) נכונו אליה : ובכל יום ויום היתה אומרת אליה׳ הנה אינך ראויה לאיש 14

ולהיות לך זרע על הארץ והנה את חושבת להרגיני כאשר הרגת אתהם: 15

ויהי היום ותעל בעלייה. ותעמד שם שלשה ימים לילה ויום. לחם לא 16

אכלה ומים לא שתתה. ותעמד לפני יהוה בתפילה ובתחנונים להנקם מן 17

האמה ההיא המחרפת אותה: ותחשב להמית את עצמה לולי כי 18

יראה פן תורד שיבת אביה בינון שאולה ופן יאמרו קטיהם לשמצה. בת 19

אחת היתה לו יחידה ותמת את עצמה: ויהי כאשר תמו שלשת הימים 20

ותפל ותתחנן לפני יהוה ותאמר: ברוך יהוה אלהים אלהי ישראל שומר 21

הברית והחסד לשמרי בריתו ולאהבי מצותיו⁷ : אתה הוא העונה בעת 22

צרה פודה ומציל ומושיע. גומל לחייבים טובות: אליך נשאתי עיני 23

היושבי בשמים. כי ידעתי כי עפר אנכי ואל עפר אשוב : והנה 17

אנכי מתפללת לפניך ומפלת תחנתי (על?) אשר חרפוני חגם : והנה ידעת 18

את לבבי כי לא חמדתי איש. ומהורה אנכי בעמדי לפניך: במושב 19

לצים לא ישבתי. ועם משחקים לא באתי. ועם פעלי און לא הלכתי. ולא 20

חפצתי איש כי אם ביראתך (!) . ואנכי לא הייתי נכונה להם: ואני ידעתי 20

כי איש אחד הת..ת.(!) לי והוכחת לי. ואם רצונך שלחיהו לי. כי זאת 21

תורת האדם העובדך באמת ואחריתו תקוה : (.1 לתת לו אחרית ותקוה)⁸ 21

ובבא עליו צרה וצוקה והצלתו בצדקתך. כי לא תחפוץ במות המת כי 22

אם בשובם מדרכו וחיה⁹. והצדקה תעביר רוע הנזירה: יהי שמך 22

מבורך מעולם ועד עולם אמן:¹⁰ בעת ההיא נשמע צעקתה עם צעקת 23

---

1 cf. Zech. 7, 9. Ps. 25, 10. 2 cf. Ps. 106, 4 and The additional
service for New Moon in the Liturgy. 3 cf. Ps. 77, 8. 4 cf. Deut. 28, 37.
5 I. Sam. 1, 6. 6 Ezra 9, 2. 7 Deut. 7, 9.
9 Liturgy of the Day of Atonement; v. Ezek. 18, 33 and 33, 11.
10 cf. Ps. 113, 2.

יהודה בבשת פנים על המכה אשר הכהו אלהים· על אשר חירף וגידף·

15 ויכנע סנחריב· ויך רבים מישראל· וטובי היה קוברם: ויוגד למלך· ויצו

16 המלך להרוג אותו ולשלול כל אשר לו: ויברח טובי הוא ואשתו ובניו
וילכו יחפים וערומים בלי כסות בקרח ובלי מחיה. ובכל (!) אשר הלך מצא

17 אוהבים רבים: ויהי מקץ ארבעים וחמשה ימים הרגו סנחריב בניו

II. אסרחדון(!) ושראצר· וישמע טובי וישב אל ביתו וכל שללו הושב לו : II. ויהי
1,2 אחריכן ויהי חג י"י· ויעש טובי סעודה גדולה בביתו: ויאמר אל טוביה
בני· בני לך והבא לנו אנשים ממשפחתינו יראי אלהים ויאכלו עמנו :

3 וילך טוביה. וישב ויגד לאביו· כי אחד מבני ישראל ראה הרוג ומושלך

4 בחוץ : ויקם טובי מכסאו ויעזב הסעודה ולא אכל· וילך אל המת וישאהו

5 בסתר אל ביתו · ובבא השמש קברהו· ואחר אכל באבל ורעדה: ויזכר
את הדבר אשר ביד עמוס הנביא· והפכתי את חגיכם לאבל ושיריכם

6 לקינה‏[1]: וידיבו אותו קרוביו לאמר הנה ידעת כי צוה המלך להרגך
על אשר קברת המתים ותברח ותגצל נפשך· ועודך מחזיק בתומתך‏[2]:

7 ויאמר· הנה הרבה יראתי את אדני האדנים מיראתי את המלך קרוץ

8 מחומר‏[3] כמוני· וטובי היה הולך ושוב אחרי ההרוגים· ובסתר היה מביאם

9 וקוברם בחצות הלילה: ויהי היום ויעף טובי מקבור אותם· ולא טבל

10 ידיו ובמים לא שטפם אחרי קוברו אותם : וישכב על המטה אצל הקיר
וישן· והנה קן צפור דרור ויפל על עיניו צאתם ותכחין עיניו ולא ראה.

11 ולבעבור נסותו עשה לו האלהים כל זאת כאשר עשה לאיוב‏[4]: וטובי
היה ירא את יהוה מנעוריו· וכל (ובכל ‏1.) זאת לא נתן טובי תפלה לאלהים‏[4]

12 וידבק באלהי ישראל ויבטח בחסדו : ויבאו לפגיו ריעי איוב אליפז התימני
ובלדד השוחי וצופר הנעמתי· ויהיו כולם מלעינים עליו לאמר· (איה) צדקתך
אשר בטחת בה לאמר· צדקתי ואקבר את המתים ואנמול להם חסד‏[5]?:

13 וינער בהם טובי ויאמר· אמגם זך וחף אנכי וצדקתי תעגה בי‏[6]· והנה גם
הרע וגם הטוב נקבל באהבה ובשמחה לבב‏[7]· כי כל משפטי יהוה ישרים‏[8]:

14 כי כל אשר אמונתו שלימה לא ימיר ולא יחליף· ונתן לו אלהים חיי

15 העולם הבא : ותהי אשתו חכמת לב לעשות כל מלאכת מחשבת·

16 ותעש לרבים ותכלכל אישה במעשה ידיה : והנה בכל (!) יום קבלה שעיר

17 עזים אחד בשכרה ותביאהו אל הבית· והשעיר הולך וגעה בבית : וישמע
טובי קול השעיר ויאמר לה· ראה פן גניבה אתך· השב תשיב אותו לבעליו·

18 כי כן צונו אלהינו ולא נוכל להלינו בביתינו ולקחת לנו : ותען ותאמר· אם
צדיק אתה כדבריך· מדוע קראתך כל הצרה הזאת? כה משפטה כל הימים

III. לדבר אתו קשות עד כי קץ בחייו : III. ויהי כשמע טובי הנאצות האלה
1 ויאנח וישבר לבו וישם פניו· אל הקיר ויתפלל בדמעות· ויאמר· ויהוה צדיק

---

1 Amos 8, 10.   2 Job 2, 9.   3 Job 33, 6.   4 Job 1, 22.
5 cf. Job 33, 9.   6 Gen. 30, 33.   7 Job 2, 10.   8 cf. Nehem. 9, 13.